85 NORTH

85 NORTH

BOBBY NASH

Falstaff Books
Charlotte, North Carolina

ALSO BY BOBBY NASH

NOVELS
Evil Ways
Deadly Games!
Snow Falls
Snow Storm
Earthstrike Agenda
Domino Lady "Money Shot"
Alexandra Holzer's Ghost Gal: The Wild Hunt
Fightcard: Barefoot Bones

SHORT FICTION
Zombies Vs. Robots: No Man's Land
Green Hornet Casefiles
Green Hornet: Still at Large
The Big Bad
The Ruby Files
Lance Star: Sky Ranger
The Spider: Extreme Prejudice

COMIC BOOKS/GRAPHIC NOVELS
Edgar Rice Burroughs' At The Earth's Core
Domino Lady: Threesome
Operation: Silver Moon
Lance Star: Sky Ranger "One Shot!"
Demonslayer

See a full list of titles at www.bobbynash.com.

CONTENTS

FOREWORD

We all have them.

If you work as a writer long enough, you will find yourself with a drawer (or computer file folder) full of unused stories that, for one reason or another, found themselves without a home. Sometimes that comes from rejection, other times it comes from projects stalling or publishers going out of business or even just things falling by the wayside.

Whatever the reason, things happen and some stories fall through the cracks.

When Fallstaff Books head honcho, John Hartness asked me if I had any stories lying around that needed a home, it did not take long to dig up enough stories to fill this volume.

The stories in this volume were all written for anthologies for a variety of publishers over the last ten years or so that, for one reason or another, have not seen print. There are three exceptions to that in these tales, but the rest are seeing print here for the first time.

For a moment, I had the urge to update these tales, to give them a modern pass, but outside of editing notes, I resisted the urge. These tales are a product of when they were written and where I, as a writer, was at the time.

The stories in this volume cover a ranch of genres, which is part of the appeal of working in anthologies. Writing a short story allows the author to play in genres that he or she may not get to write on a regular basis.

85 North is loosely based on a true story that happened to some friends and I on a long stretch of Interstate 85 North above Charlotte, NC. I gave it a bit of a sci-fi twist. The horror elements were real. I still get chills thinking about it.

Moon Girl: Blood Moon puts the public domain comic book character in dire straits when she is pulled out of her own time into the middle of a paranormal feud deep in the past. Can she stop the fighting and get back to where she belongs?

Beyond The Horizon was a journey into fantasy for me. A young boy looks tot he horizon and wonders what, if anything, exists beyond the mountains that make surround his village. Against all advice, he decides to find out.

Magnus: The Apprentice tells the beginning of a teenage magician's quest to stop an evil magical being from taking over the world.

Gypsy is the story of a young woman who has had enough. She creates a super hero identity for herself and goes out to reclaim her neighborhood from those who would threaten it.

Primal Instincts introduces us to Dr. Petra Alexander, who has come to a place known only as the river when the local animal population begins acting out of character. Does the local dam have something to do with the animal's wild behavior and can they stop whatever is causing it before the animals kill everything in their path?

Showdown at Broken Eagle is the oldest story in this collection. It originally started as a 3 part comic book story for an anthology, but has been adapted to prose. Broken Eagle is a one-horse western town. It's like something out of a movie, but this town has a secret. Three strangers come to town just as a sinister force awakens outside of town. The original inhabitants of Broken Ridge have returned… and they want their town back.

The Sentinels: The Road To Hell features Blitzkrieg, a character from Van Allen Plexico's Sentinels novels. Blitzkrieg is an assassin, but has orders not to take any outside contracts. Bored, he decides to ignore that order and take a freelance contract. That's when things go wrong.

Big thanks to John, Jay, and Jaym at Fallstaff Books for putting this collection of stories together. I'm happy to see them get into reader's hands after all this time.

I'd also like to offer a big thank you to the publishers who had originally ordered these stories for giving me permission to take them back for this collection. Much appreciated.

Also, thanks to you for picking up this collection of odds and ends. I do appreciate it and hope you enjoy the stories.

Happy Reading.

Bobby Nash
Somewhere just off 85 North

85 NORTH

Loosely Based on a True Story.

PETE JENNINGS WAS LOOKING FORWARD TO COLLEGE.
He, along with Robert Schultz and Bethany Hopkins -- three of the four musketeers from Sommersville High -- would be attending the University of Georgia come fall. He was happy to know that two of his best friends would be on campus with him because he could not imagine what life would be like without hanging out with the high school sweethearts on a regular basis. They had been the best of friends and almost inseparable since meeting on the playground in elementary school.

Jill Daughtridge was a different matter. Pete had been in love with her since he first laid eyes on her the day she and her family moved in across the street from him when they were in middle school. Of course, he never once told her of his feelings, especially once they became friends. Jill was popular with everyone: head cheerleader, voted most likely to succeed, Valedictorian of their graduating class, and way out of Pete's league.

All through high school she had dated one football player after another, much to the love-struck Pete's chagrin. If there was one thing Pete was most certainly not, it was athletic. His idea of an exciting Friday night involved the Syfy Channel and a meat lover's. His friends often teased him good-naturedly about his fascination with his favorite science fiction show, *Star Trek*. Before they started high school, Robert had called his friend "Spock." Once they started high school, Robert had dropped the nickname, at least publicly. But high school was behind them now and they were starting new chapters in their lives. Pete wanted to have Jill as part of his chapter as something more than just a friend.

He summoned up his courage.

Now that they were starting their new post-high school lives, he was going to ask her out.

Before that happened, however, she dropped a bombshell that shattered his plans into a million tiny pieces. Jill had been accepted to Harvard University with a full scholarship. It was a fantastic accomplishment and she was excited and ready to dive into her studies. Pete was excited for her too, but the thought of her moving to Boston while he remained in Georgia broke his fragile heart.

Robert and Bethany, seeking to lift their friend's mood, asked Jill to accompany them to UGA to check out their new place before she headed off to Cambridge. One final blowout, they called it. She accepted.

Pete knew it was his last chance.

They hit the town with gusto, moving from club to club, listening to the bands playing live music while they danced, laughed, and drank the night away, thanks to the flask Pete smuggled in and Bethany's bottle of "water" that was actually filled with vodka from her parents' liquor cabinet. They had finally settled at a newly-opened club called The Sidewinder. The club was new, but it had a retro feel that harked back to the clubs of Athens' musical heyday. Two bands from Gwinnett County were on the bill tonight and both played very well. The joint, as they said in old movies, was jumping.

Around midnight, the sound of sirens cut through the din, filling the night air, as an ambulance pulled to the curb outside. Like many of the other patrons, the foursome ran outside to see what all the commotion was about. They watched as paramedics leapt from their rig to help an older gentleman who was lying on the ground, clutching at his chest. A crowd quickly formed a semicircle around the scene.

"What's going on?" Pete asked one of the bystanders.

"Some old guy had a heart attack."

"Is he okay?" Bethany wondered aloud.

"Who knows," the bystander said. "Not even sure what he was doing here. He'd been sitting out here for a while. Guess he couldn't handle the music," he said unsympathetically before heading back into the club.

"That poor man," Jill said, remembering her father's painful experience a year earlier.

"Yeah. It's sad," Pete said, motioning them back toward the entrance. "Come on, let's get back inside before we lose our table."

The rest of the night was a blur. The four friends laughed and told stories, then laughed some more. It was a perfect night and the friends were happy they had decided to have one last big party as a send-off. Just before dawn, as they were walking back to Robert and Bethany's apartment, Pete made a suggestion that would have an irreversible impact on each of their lives.

"Why don't we drive Jill up to Boston?" he suggested.

Jill laughed away the suggestion. "That's sweet," she said, "but you don't have to do that. I know you've got a lot to do here before classes start."

Knowing his friend's feelings for Jill, Robert stepped in before Pete could agree with her and back out of the trip. "No. It sounds like a great idea to me," he said. "What do you think, Beth?"

"Sure. Come on, Jill," Bethany urged. "It'll be fun."

"Okay," Jill said, convinced. "I guess it's settled, then."

Pete was all smiles when he shouted, "Road trip!"

Pete woke at a few minutes after two in the afternoon.

The last thing he remembered was watching the sun come up from the roof of Robert and Beth's apartment building. He couldn't recall how he made it back to the apartment, but he assumed he must have, since he woke up on the couch. The others were all up and ready for the trip, which was understandable. None of them had drunk quite as much as Pete had the night before. He was happy they let him sleep in.

Pete was not a morning person -- or an early afternoon person in this case. He mumbled an all-but-unintelligible greeting as he crossed the apartment toward the bathroom with a towel draped over his shoulder, his eyes barely open and his mouth feeling as though it was full of cotton. Pete hopped in the shower and let the steamy water wash over him while his friends finished packing the car. He was never on time for anything. If there was one constant in the universe, it was that Pete Jennings was running late. It was not one of his more promising attributes, but his friends had come to accept it, if not appreciate it.

By the time Pete emerged from the bathroom he looked more or less like his usual self, although he looked a bit more tired than usual. A quick bite to eat of something easily microwaveable and he was ready to hit the road.

"Always have to wait on somebody," Jill ribbed him good-naturedly as they piled into Robert's new Chevy Equinox. Robert and Bethany were in front and Pete and Jill in the back. Robert and Bethany were doing everything they could to make it easy for Pete to profess his feelings for Jill. The only thing that could get in the way was Pete's own fear.

"Har-de-har-har," Pete replied sarcastically, as he usually did when they remarked on his tardy nature. He countered with his usual "are we there yet?" before they even made it out of the apartment complex.

No one laughed.

The drive to Boston was quite a long one so Bethany and Jill had stocked the cooler with drinks, snacks, sandwich fixings, and plenty of bottled water. They decided to play it by ear on where they were going to stop for the night, or if they even needed to stop. Switching out drivers might allow for a straight drive with no stopovers. If they needed to sleep they would find a hotel off the interstate.

And they were off.

It took about an hour for them to reach the interstate. Athens, while a great college town, was basically smack dab in the middle of nowhere. Once you got out of town there was nothing but country roads and small towns where the speed limit dropped dramatically to a brake-riding twenty-five miles per hour, which afforded plenty of sightseeing opportunities.

Once they hit Interstate 85 North, Robert got it up to seventy-five, just a few miles per hour above the posted limit of seventy. After getting a ticket for speeding on his last trip through South Carolina, he kept the speed respectable. Better safe than sorry. The last thing he wanted to discuss with his dad was why the insurance bill had risen again. So, cruising along, it took a little less than two hours before Georgia faded in the rearview mirror and they crossed into South Carolina.

Robert slowed back to the speed limit, referring to The Palmetto State as one big speed trap.

Still exhausted, Pete did not remember much after that, as he fell back asleep, his head resting against the window. Before his eyes closed and he drifted away, he hoped he didn't drool in front of Jill, or else he might die of embarrassment.

Pete woke with a jolt.

"Whasgoin'on?' he mumbled.

"Good evening, sleepy head," Jill said with a sweet, playful smile.

"Hi," Pete said sheepishly once he realized he wasn't dreaming and returned the smile. "What's going on?" he asked more clearly.

"Nothing," Robert said from behind the wheel. "It'll be dark soon so we figured we should make a gas stop while there's still a little daylight. The off ramp is a little rough though. Doesn't look like it gets much use."

"There's grass growing up through the cracks," Bethany pointed out. "Are you sure this is a real exit?"

"There was an exit sign."

From the backseat, Pete yawned. "I could use a chance to stretch the ol' legs and a bathroom break wouldn't hurt either," he said.

They pulled off the off-ramp and followed the road across an old bridge, before coming to a dead end in front of a small service station with an attached diner. There were only a couple of cars in the parking lot, none of them newer than a decade or two old. The diner itself looked as if its best days were behind it. The building itself was in desperate need for a fresh coat of paint.

As Robert topped off the tank, the others stretched out the kinks from the three and a half hours on the road. Thankfully, Robert's SUV wasn't as cramped as a smaller car, but after a few hours, even it became uncomfortable.

"I've got to hit the bathroom," Pete said.

"Me too," Robert said as he replaced the gas cap. "Can you pay for this?" he asked Bethany as he handed her a few bills.

"Sure," she said.

Robert jogged to catch up with Pete before he reached the entrance to the gas station. "So, how's it going with you two lovebirds," he asked playfully as they opened the door. "Is your master plan working? I think she found your snoring adorable."

"Oh, shut up."

"Bathrooms?" Robert asked the older lady with the sour expression behind the counter. Without looking at either of them, she chucked a thumb in the direction of the diner. He could hear the low murmur of conversation and the clinking of metal utensils against plastic plates, and could smell a greasy aroma that reminded him of a cook-out coming from that direction.

Robert thanked her, but the lady had already lost interest in them, if she had even noticed they were there. As he rounded the corner into the diner, Robert saw Bethany come in alone to pay for the gas. Jill was outside, punching a number into her cell phone.

"Smells good," Pete said as the guys stepped into the noisy diner.

They were greeted with silence.

All eyes were on them as they stepped into the diner, but none of the patrons moved a muscle or made a sound. If not for the eyes that followed them, it might have appeared as if they were made of stone.

Pete found the silence eerily unnerving.

From the look of it, they could have stepped back in time. The diner was filled with weathered faces that had spent a lot of time in the sun. From the way most of them were dressed, the guys assumed they were farmers, although neither one of them knew of any farms in the area. Some wore jeans and flannel shirts while others sported overalls and each table had some kind of hat sitting on it. Most of the diner's patrons were men, but there were a few women present. The guys noticed a distinct lack of business people. Only one of them wore a suit and it looked like he had been wearing it for years. He sat off in the back corner alone and had been reading a folded newspaper before the guys walked in.

Robert and Pete both offered friendly smiles as they walked the length of the diner with booths on either side. Both of them could feel the eyes of the patrons on them. Self-conscious, they picked up the pace and walked a little faster.

Once inside the bathroom, Robert let out a sigh of relief.

"What the hell was that?" Pete said. "I feel like I should be looking for pods under their seats."

Robert laughed it off, but he too felt weird. "The sad part is we get to walk out there again to get back to the car."

"Oh, fun. Too bad there's not a window we can crawl out."

Robert laughed.

Pete decided to forego drying his hands on the stained antique cloth roll towel and used his jeans as a towel. Robert did likewise.

The patrons continued staring at them until they once again were back in the gas station side. Behind them, the guys heard the murmuring and clinking of utensils on plates resume once they were out of sight.

Pete let out a breath. "What say we get the hell out of here?"

"I like that plan. This place gives me the creeps."

Back behind the wheel, Robert told the girls about his and Pete's experience in the diner as he pulled back onto the road.

"That's nothing," Bethany said. "I asked the lady behind the counter how far it is to High Top and she said she'd never heard of it. I know we have to be close."

"Did you notice the music rack? There's not a single CD in the place. Everything was on cassette tapes. Who uses cassette tapes anymore?" Robert said.

"Weird. I'm just glad we got out of there before one of them pulled out a banjo and started playing the theme to *Deliverance*," Pete joked.

"Where's the on ramp?" Robert asked from the driver's seat.

"That's not very funny," Jill said.

"I'm not kidding. We've been driving for a couple minutes. It didn't take that long to get to the gas station."

"Did you pass it? It's getting dark. Maybe there's no sign."

"I guess that's possible," Robert said, even thought he did not believe it.

"Turn around," Jill suggested, nervousness in her voice.

"Good idea."

Robert turned the car around, which wasn't an easy feat on the tiny stretch of pavement. They each kept an eye peeled for the on-ramp or the bridge, but there was nothing. A couple minutes later they were once again approaching a familiar landmark, though not the one they were hoping to see.

"Is that…?"

"Okay, this is a little weird," Robert muttered.

"We're back at the diner," Pete groused. "Maybe we can ask for directions."

"Maybe," Robert said as he pulled into the now empty parking lot. "Something's not right here. Why are all of the lights out?"

After putting the car in park under the only functioning light in the lot – near the gas pumps – Robert and the others stepped out into the cool evening air. The setting sun on the horizon cast deep, menacing shadows that played across everything. The light near the pumps was on the verge of dying and it flickered on and off.

They walked back to the front door of the diner they had been standing in not ten minutes earlier only to find it boarded up.

"Spooky," Pete said as he tried to look through the window that was caked with dirt. "This place looks like it's been closed for years. It doesn't make any sense. We were just here a couple minutes ago." He wiped at the window with his hand to try to clean it enough to see inside. All he could see was that it was dark.

Robert tried the door to the gas station. The sign hanging on the inside of the glass showed CLOSED. The door was locked and the handles were coated in rust. He was certain they had not been in such a rundown condition earlier.

Jill asked the question that was on each of their minds. "Where did everybody go?"

"I'd really like to leave now," Bethany told Robert.

"Good plan," he agreed.

They turned and each of them stopped dead in their tracks.

"Where's my car?"

The parking lot was empty.

"Where's your car?"

Robert was angry. "Alright," he shouted to whoever was out there playing this stupid prank on them. "Very funny! Ha! Ha! Good one! Whoever you are you'd better bring my damned car back right this minute or we're going to have a problem! Do you hear me?"

Only the sound of insects answered.

"And just what are we supposed to do now?" Bethany asked.

"I'm scared," Jill muttered.

"It's okay," Pete said as he put an arm around her shoulder to calm her. It didn't help.

"Any ideas?" Bethany asked.

"We could walk to the interstate and flag down some help."

"I can't see any lights from the expressway," said Pete. "And I don't hear any cars, do you?"

Robert shook his head. The only sounds were those of the insects living in the woods and a rustle of leaves.

The rustle got louder.

As one, the four teens turned back toward the diner.

Or what was left of it.

What remained of the diner was a burnt husk. The scent of burnt wood was faint, but noticeable.

"Uh..." Pete started.

"What the hell?" Jill said, continuing her friend's train of thought. "There's no way this just happened."

"No way," Robert agreed as he reached out to touch the charred remains of the diner's outer wall. His hand came back with dark gray ash on it. "It's not even warm. This happened a long time ago."

"Bullshit! We were just looking at it!"

"Easy, Jill. Easy. I know, but something is definitely wrong here."

"Looks like we've been pulled out of the space-time continuum," Pete said, making a poor attempt at humor.

"That's not funny," Bethany said.

"You have a better explanation?"

No one answered.

"I didn't think so," Pete said. "Now, if we stay ... what is that?"

"What is what?"

"That!"

Pete pointed toward the woods on the far side of the diner. Moving through the thick foliage was a group of people -- at least they assumed it was a group of people. All they could see were the torches they carried. From the look of it, there were easily twenty or so torches moving through the woods.

Moving straight toward them.

"Go! Go!" Robert said as he herded his friends in the opposite direction.

"Maybe they know how to get out of here?" suggested Bethany.

"Somehow, I don't think they're coming to help us," replied Pete.

They ran to the road and dropped into the ditch that led along the far side. From there they were able to look over the edge and see who the new arrivals were, although Pete had a pretty good guess who they would see.

"How can you be so sure they won't help us?" Bethany asked Robert once they were under cover.

"Have you never watched a horror movie?" Pete asked. "They have torches! That's never a good thing."

"Do you know who they are?" Jill whispered.

"I have a suspicion…" Robert answered, trailing off without taking his eyes off the approaching strangers as they moved into the clearing that was once the diner's parking lot. "Yeah, I thought so," Robert said, acknowledging that his suspicion was correct. "Pete?"

"I see them. They're the ones who were eating breakfast in the diner."

"Yep."

"What's the plan?"

"Your guess is as good as mine, Pete."

"That's not very reassuring."

"No," Robert said. "No, it's not."

Suddenly, one of the torch wielders pointed toward them and shouted something to the others. As one, the torch-wielding mob all turned toward the friends and started heading their way.

"Dammit!" Pete shouted. "They've spotted us!"

Robert spurred them into motion with a simple, "Run!"

They ran.

The woods were thick, but manageable. Uneven ground caused them to stumble a few times, but somehow they managed to keep their balance. In the dark, tree limbs snagged clothing and bit into their skin, but the four teenagers ran for all they were worth.

Robert took the lead, trying to clear a path for the others. Bethany and Jill were only a step behind him. Pete brought up the rear, trying to keep an eye on the men and women who were after them as much as he kept watch on his friends to make sure they did not get separated. As a result, he was starting to lag behind.

The woods were larger than they had first appeared. Much like everything they had encountered since leaving the interstate, this did not make any sense. From the diner, it should have been an easy jog to the expressway, but like their car and the diner it too had vanished.

They needed a miracle to escape the woods.

Robert crashed through a thick cluster of leaves without slowing down … right into the path of a tractor trailer doing seventy-plus miles per hour.

Acting quickly, Bethany and Jill grabbed him and jerked him out of the road as the behemoth machine roared past, horn blaring into the night.

They fell to the ground at the edge of the road, hardly believing that they had found it.

"Pete!" Robert shouted as Bethany stepped out to flag down an oncoming set of headlights coming toward them. "Come on!"

An SUV slowed and pulled off the side of the road. The couple in the front rolled down the passenger window and asked if they needed help. From the look of the three of them, each dirty and covered with scrapes and cuts, they must have appeared to have been in a bad accident.

"We need a ride! Quick!" Jill told them, standing beside the car. "They're after us!"

"Who?" the woman in the passenger seat asked.

"We don't know," Jill pleaded. "Just get us out of here!"

"Get in," the driver said.

Jill shouted for Robert and Bethany to come on, but they were still waiting for Pete, who had not yet followed them out of the woods.

Robert told Bethany to go to the car. He would get Pete. As she ran to join Jill at the car, Robert ran back into the woods, but saw no sign of Pete or the people who had been chasing them. Robert shouted his friend's name, but only the noise of the insects answered him. He wanted to run back into the woods and find his friend, but then he thought of Jill and Bethany. He couldn't just abandon them either.

He would come back with the police to look for his friend.

Robert ran to the SUV and climbed into the backseat with the others. "Do you have a phone?" he asked the driver.

"Yes, but no signal. Not out here in the middle of nowhere."

"Where's Pete?" Jill asked.

"We need to get to a phone or a police station," Robert told the driver instead of answering Jill's question. "Our friend is missing and we need their help to find him."

As the car pulled away from the side of the road and sped away into the night, Robert turned and stared at the spot where he had lost his friend until they were far enough away that he could no longer see it.

"We'll come back and find him," he whispered to his friends.

"We'll find him."

The sun beat down on the asphalt as Pete burst free from the woods.

He shouted in triumph as he sank to his knees at the edge of the interstate. He had been looking for the exit for so long that he never thought he would be able to find it. Days had become weeks until he had finally lost track of time. Not that time followed any logical pattern within the void.

But finally, after all this time he had done it.

He had escaped.

He was free.

He couldn't help but laugh as he leaned against the sign that that told him where the road headed.

85 North.

After a few minutes he saw a car approach and he got to his feet and waved it down. It was an older model car, but that really didn't matter. Pete's only concern at the moment was finding his friends and letting them know he was all right. There was no way to know how much time had passed outside of the... whatever it was he was stuck in, but he felt like at least a couple of years had passed for him. Somehow, he suspected that time moved at a different speed outside of the phenomenon as it did on the inside.

He was in luck. The driver was obviously a Good Samaritan because the car's turn signal came on and the driver pulled over to the side of the interstate and stopped.

Pete ran to the passenger side as the driver leaned over and rolled down the window.

"Oh, thank God," Pete told the driver as he leaned down to look inside the car. "You're a life saver!"

"Are you okay?" the driver asked. He wore a brown business suit and burgundy tie. A leather briefcase sat in the passenger seat. An oldies channel blared from the car's antiquated stereo.

"I am now. Thank you for stopping."

"No problem," the businessman said with a friendly smile. "Were you in an accident?"

"Something like that," Pete said, preferring not to have to explain what had happened to him. He wasn't really sure he could explain it. "I've… uh, I've been walking awhile."

"Do you need a lift? Get in."

"That would be great," Pete said, smiling for the first time in ages. "But first, can I borrow your cell? I need to let my friends know I'm okay."

The driver looked at Pete oddly as he moved his briefcase to the backseat. "My what?"

"Seriously? You don't have a cell phone?" Pete said with astonishment as he got into the front seat.

"What's a cell phone?" the driver asked.

Suddenly, Pete's world turned upside down as all of the pieces came together for him. He had said it himself earlier. Time worked differently inside the anomaly the friends had encountered. He'd seen the evidence of it with his own eyes, but he never suspected, never even dreamed what might happen if he escaped through the wrong opening. The idea of multiple thresholds to cross had not even occurred to him until just that moment.

"Are you okay?"

Pete felt the blood drain from his face. He had spent so much time trying to find a way out without any thought to just where he might end up. And now that he was out he didn't know how to go back and start again. He was free, but still trapped.

"I have an odd question to ask you," he told the driver.

"Okay." The driver looked apprehensive.

"What year is this?"

"I beg your pardon?"

"I know it sounds silly, but I hit my head and I'm not sure … please, just tell me."

"Okay," the driver said, concern in his voice. "It's 1961. August 7th to be exact."

Pete felt the impact as something slammed into him from behind. It would be a few minutes before he realized that what hit him was the ground after his balance betrayed him and he dropped like a stone.

The Good Samaritan helped him into the car and offered to take him to the nearest hospital. Pete was too stunned to argue. Only one thought bounced around in his brain.

What am I going to do now?

Pete stood outside the newly opened club called The Sidewinder and wondered what he was going to do now that he was there. He had planned for this moment for years, rehearsing what he would tell them, but now that it was before him he found himself wondering what to do next.

The club was new, but had been designed to have a retro feel. Pete felt that he and the club had a lot in common. He had the unique perspective of having lived in two different eras. Living through the decades before his birth, the Sixties, Seventies, and Eighties had been an experience he cherished. It was especially exciting to see the original Star Trek series during its initial run and he got to see Star Wars on the big screen in its original, unaltered form. The geek in him loved the opportunities with which he had been presented.

The downside was living through some turbulent times in the Sixties when protests and anti-war demonstrations that he had only read about as a kid were happening all around him. He tried to help when he could, to warn those that would listen when he remembered something from his history books as a kid, but sadly no one seemed all that interested in hearing his words. He wondered if he would have believed what he was saying if he didn't have the foreknowledge of the world's events. Somehow, he suspected, he wouldn't have.

His life had become a living education, but the human part of him missed what could have been. The defining moment of his life was just ahead of him. At sixty-nine years old he had lived a wonderful life, but he always wondered how things might have turned out if he had not suggested that one last road trip.

That thought had haunted his sleep for decades.

With the fateful day fast approaching, he knew it was time to act. There would be only one shot at putting it right. If he could just stop it from happening, then perhaps he would get his happily ever after.

He sat on a park bench across the street from the club and listened as two bands from out of town played. Pete recalled enjoying their music when he was a kid, but the names of each escaped him at the moment. It had been almost fifty years since he had last heard them, after all. He wondered if either of the bands had found success outside of the college bar scene.

The joint, as they used to say in old movies, was jumping.

He had considered going inside, but despite having the hearing aid turned to its lowest setting, the music was just a bit too loud for him these days. It made him feel old.

And that's when he saw them.

He recognized them easily, even though it had been well over forty years since he had last seen them. Robert, Bethany, and Jill looked just the way he remembered. Seeing them brought a flood of memories back to him. He remembered the good times, the bad, and his intense feelings for Jill. After all this time the fire still burned for her. One look at her across the way and Pete knew that he had to stop it all from happening. If not for his sake, then he would do it for Jill. He could not bear to lose her a second time.

The future could be changed. He believed it with every fiber of his being.

He watched his friends enter the club.

"It's now or never," Pete whispered and he stood, holding onto a lamppost for support.

On unsteady legs, Pete started slowly across the street, once again cursing the ailments that wracked his body of late.

He stopped just outside the door and felt the music pounding against him in waves.

He was so close.

So close.

So…

And then he felt it.

The pounding.

It was a familiar sensation, one he had experienced twice a decade before, one that remained fresh in his memory. Much like he had at age fifty and fifty-six, Pete winced as a vice gripped his heart, the organ beating loudly even as it felt like it was being clenched tightly by an enormous fist.

"Heart… attack," he whispered as his legs buckled underneath him and he fell to the concrete sidewalk. "No."

All other sounds faded beneath the thunderous pounding of his heart, beating so loud that his eardrums threatened to burst if the noise level did not subside. He felt hands on him, heard unintelligible sounds that he assumed belonged to the concerned people who were leaning over him. He tried to speak, but his body refused to cooperate. Nothing worked.

The sound of sirens cut through the thundering, but only barely. An ambulance pulled to the curb and the paramedics leapt out of their rig to try and help him. Pete tried to explain, but no one could hear him.

Lying on the ground, clutching at his chest, Pete noticed the crowd form around him as the curious and concerned stopped to see what was going on. The crowd quickly formed a semicircle around the scene.

And that's when he saw them.

He saw his oldest friends, Robert, Bethany, and Jill standing there along with his younger self and he remembered this scene. He remembered the old man being taken away in the ambulance and that was when he knew that it had all been for naught. As he was loaded into the back of the ambulance, Pete screamed their names, but knew that they would not hear him.

He had failed.

There was no way to keep them safe.

There was no way to save his future.

It was all going to happen again.

And again.

And again.

And ag…

As the ambulance pulled away into the night, Pete cried in frustration and pain, knowing that he had failed and that it would all happen again just as it had before. The tightness in his chest increased and Pete realized that his time was up.

"Time to go," a tiny singsong voice whispered in his ear.

As he felt his heart's last beat, Pete saw an angel hovering above him. She was lovely and reminded him of Jill. The angel smiled. She told him that it was time and asked if he was ready to go.

He was and he told her so.

The angel smiled down at him as she reached out a hand.

He took it.

Pete couldn't help but laugh as the angel said the last thing he expected to ever hear again.

"Road trip."

VAN ALLEN PLEXICO'S SENTINELS
THE ROAD TO HELL

1.

KARL KOENIG WAS HAVING A BAD DAY.

Nothing had gone right since that botched mission in Sarajevo. Not that the mission's failure was in any way his fault. Koenig's boss, The Field Marshal, had decided to take it out on him anyway. Being the good, loyal soldier he was, Koenig listened to his commander's rant without interruption, but he felt his blood boiling beneath the surface.

The Field Marshal was under extreme pressure from those above him in the food chain; yet one more thing that rubbed Koenig the wrong way. Before they had been brought to this dimension everything had seemed so simple and straightforward.

Koenig liked simple.

There was an order to things and that's just the way he liked it.

Of course, since coming here things had changed. No longer was the Field Marshal making all of the decisions. Now he reported to another man, an American no less, named Jameson. Koenig did not trust Jameson. The man clearly had his own agenda.

Koenig planned to keep an eye on him.

The Field Marshal ended his tirade with a blunt "Dismissed!" No matter which dimension you called your home, in military circles that meant, "*Get out!*"

Koenig left, slamming the door behind him. It was a small act of rebellion, but it

felt good nonetheless. Not good enough to settle his irritated nerves, but it was a start. What he needed at the moment was to blow off a little steam.

And he knew just the place to do it.

He stepped inside the room and allowed himself a thin smile.

Though this was not the type of establishment he often frequented, Koenig knew it well. It was a valuable resource for the free flow of information almost as much as a place where alcoholic beverages of the watered-down variety also flowed freely.

The place had no official name.

There was no sign on the window sporting a fancy logo. Only an old flashing neon signed flashed the word BAR in a pale electric blue. Koenig chuckled at the private joke each and every time he saw the gaudy sign flash blue. Below it was another neon sign of a newer vintage that simply added OPEN.

Some patrons began referring to the place as The Open Bar.

The name stuck.

Koenig waved away the smoke that assailed him the instant he stepped inside. He had never seen the inside of the bar without the ever-present layer, a mixture of cheap cigarettes, cigars, imported cigars, and sweat. It was an odor one never quite adjusted to smelling.

The sweat primarily came from the dancers on the small stage near the back. A DJ who believed he was far too hip for the bar had long since given up on playing to the crowd and simply played the music and introduced the girls.

A rather exotic woman Koenig had never seen before was on the stage, her silky black hair flailing wildly as she twirled around and around the dull brass pole. Koenig stood and watched her for a moment.

He did not smile.

A shame, he thought. *If only she were blonde.*

As he watched her spin and twirl, his eyes also swept the room.

Eventually, he found a familiar face and made his way across the floor, stopping long enough to slide a twenty dollar bill to the dancer. She took the money with a practiced smile and enticing wink.

Koenig did not return her smile, but one corner of his mouth rose in a knowing thin-lipped grin. That was all he was willing to give. Considering his mood, she was lucky to get that much from him.

He kept his eyes on the room as he walked. The Open Bar was considered a "safe zone" for those in the business, but one could never be too careful. Who knew how many enemies might be sitting in this very room just waiting for him to make a mistake?

Unfortunately, any waiting for such an opportunity were in for a long wait. Karl Koenig was not a man prone to making mistakes.

"Hello, Lennie," he said in his heavily accented English as he slid inside a booth along the far wall, concealed in the shadows.

Lennie Casper was a small man who seemed nervous each time Koenig saw him. Once he had wondered if it was his presence that made the little man nervous, but he was assured that such was not the case. Nervous was a permanent state of mind for Lennie Casper.

Being a facilitator was not an easy job and Lennie was considered by many to be one of the best. He had no ties to any one organization so he was approached by, and had performed services for, all sides at one time or another. As such, he was in the eternally sticky situation of being caught in the middle of things if it all hit the fan.

However, he knew where most of the bodies were buried.

And he knew who pulled the trigger in most cases.

If knowledge was indeed power, then Lennie Casper was the strongest man in the room.

"Blitzkrieg," Lennie said, a big smile on his cherub face. "It's been awhile."

Koenig removed his sunglasses.

"Yes. How is business, Lennie?"

"Oh, you know," the little man shrugged. "The usual."

Koenig grunted.

"So, is this a business or social call?"

"Business."

"Anyone I know?"

Koenig raised an eyebrow.

"I beg your pardon?"

"The mark. We taking out anyone I know? I have to protect myself, you know. These are difficult times, I'm sure you understand."

"I think you misunderstand my intentions, Lennie."

"Oh?"

Koenig noticed the facilitator's nervousness crank up a notch.

"I'm looking for..." the tall German looked around the room to make sure no one was watching.

"Yes?"

"An assignment. I'm looking for an assignment."

"You?" Lennie asked, hardly believing his ears.

"Yes."

"I'm honored. It's not often the Field Marshal seeks my..."

Koenig leaned forward and dropped his voice to a menacing octave.

"This is not for the Field Marshal. This is for me. I need an assignment."

"Ah, I see," Lennie said, a skittish grin on his face.

"And this has to remain between us."

"Okay. I get it. You need to let off a little stress or maybe you just need a little extra in the bank this month. I get it. I do. I think I've got just the thing for you. Yeah. I think you'll like this. I was kinda saving this one for Killshot Austin."

Koenig bristled at the name. Heironymous Jessup Austin was something of a legend in certain circles. Personally, Koenig could not stand the man. He behaved as if he were nobility, but was little more than a street urchin with a talent for wholesale slaughter. Koenig also doubted that Heironymous was his actual name. Probably something he stole from the painter of the same name because it made him sound more upper class than the simple Jessup Austin. The nickname Killshot was well earned. Even Koenig had to admit that the man was one hell of a shot.

"But I think I can trust you to pull it off," Lennie continued, oblivious to Koenig's utter contempt for Killshot Austin.

This time the facilitator glanced around the room to make sure no one was paying attention to their conversation.

"There's been a contract put out on someone over at the DOD."

"Department of Defense."

"Very good, Blitzkrieg. Yes. The Department of Defense."

"Wouldn't happen to be a guy named Jameson, would it?"

"Uh, no," Lennie said.

"Damn. That one I might have done for free."

"Well, if he ever makes my list I know who to call. The Senate Oversight Committee has tasked Senator Kenneth Washburn from Georgia with reviewing something called Project Three Twelve Omega."

"What is that?"

"Beats the hell out of me," Lennie said. "It's not my business to know so I don't know. Suffice it to say that someone is worried that this hayseed is going to uncover a dirty little secret or two."

"Hayseed?"

Lennie waved the question away.

"Never mind. Look, do you want the job or not?"

"I'll take it."

"Good," Lennie said, leaning back in his seat.

It was the calmest Karl Koenig had ever seen the little man. Having seen the man relax a bit it seemed oddly disconcerting to see him in any other emotional state.

"When can you start?" Lennie asked.

"I can start immediately."

2.

THE FOLLOWING THREE DAYS WERE BUSY.

So busy in fact that, despite his assurances to the contrary, Karl Koenig was not able to start immediately. Lennie was understandably less than thrilled with the delay, but he was willing to let the matter slide because he knew Koenig's record. The job would be done.

The Field Marshal was once again his normally rational self. He had tasked Blitzkrieg with an assignment that sent him out of the country.

The mission was a complete success, naturally, but he could not stop thinking about the contract on Washburn's life.

The trip home had its fair share of unexpected headaches, however.

Through what he could only assume was an eternal streak of impossibly bad luck, Koenig found himself face to face once again with that damned fool Ultraa. A tense moment that could have escalated quickly was diffused when Blitzkrieg opted for a strategic withdrawal. Retreating was tough decision, but a necessary one.

Exhausted from his mission, Koenig knew he was in no shape to go toe to toe with the costumed do-gooder so he chose the better part of valor and fled.

Wisely, he left the details of the encounter out of his official report.

After delivering his report, Koenig was dismissed and returned to his apartment. The place wasn't much, but it had become home since arriving in this dimension.

Not that he would ever admit it, but Koenig missed his homeland. In an effort to relieve his misery, he had even visited the Germany of this world shortly after his arrival, but it was not the same. The Fatherland's histories were completely divergent from one another. Even the areas that looked the same were somehow strangely different.

When he left, it was with a vow never to return. The land there held nothing for him.

As he suspected, there were numerous messages from Lennie on his machine, each one cryptic. The Facilitator was too smart to leave any incriminating evidence on an answering machine.

He sighed. There was no sense putting it off any longer. He had taken an off the books assignment and there was no turning back from it. The upside to his encounter with his hated foe was that he mood was once more in the toilet.

Karl Koenig was a professional.

He would honor his commitments.

Tonight, a man would lose his life.

And Blitzkrieg would be the one pulling the trigger.

Senator Kenneth Washburn was not what Koenig expected.

The man was short, an estimation of five feet, six inches would have been generous. The man was overweight, which did nothing to help the height issue. He was, however, well dressed. The suit he wore cost thousands easily and his hair, though thinning, was immaculately groomed. He imagined the cut set the taxpayers back a few hundred dollars.

Karl Koenig watched through the rifle scope as the honorable Senator from Georgia stepped out of his chauffeur-driven town car, buttoning his coat as he did so. The doorman bowed slightly and flashed a smile that was undoubtedly reserved for high profile guests, a description that certainly fit the rotund little man.

The Senator's arrogance made Koenig want to vomit.

He had dealt with men like the target all of his life. The very notion of power went directly to their head, erasing all reason and skewing their moral fiber at the same time. No matter how powerful men like Washburn became, they did not know what true power was.

Karl Koenig understood true power.

He was power.

He felt the familiar tingling sensation as tendrils of electrical energy danced along his skin the hair on his arms rising to attention as the power rippled outward from him.

No, the Senator did not know real power.

But that was about to change. He and power were about to receive a personal introduction.

Koenig watched as his target was escorted to one of the restaurant's best tables. He had a clear shot through the window, which was not the reason the restaurant seated such an honorable guest within plain view. They wanted to show off their famous clientele.

Unfortunately, the distinguished gentleman from Georgia had other plans.

He wanted a table in the back, far away from prying eyes.

That's when Koenig lost sight of his mark.

"Time for Plan B," he whispered as he gently returned the high-powered rifle to its case.

Before he could move, however, something else caught his eye.

"The hell?" he whispered.

Another town car had arrived, similar in design to the one that had dropped off the Senator. Given the nature of his target, it seemed understandable that one elected official might choose to meet with another out in the open. Had it not been for one little detail Koenig would not have given the car more than a cursory look.

"Scheiße!"

He knew the passenger.

"Jameson," he said through grit teeth, his anger growing.

"What are you doing here?"

3.

EVERYTHING HAD CHANGED.

Jameson's arrival suddenly put a whole new spin on things. From personal experience, Koenig knew that Jameson was not someone to be taken lightly. He had earned his place among the upper echelon of the United States Defense Department through cunning and manipulation. The man understood how to play the game that was politics and he was a very skilled competitor. Backdoor deals were not unheard of in political circles. The fact that Koenig and the Field Marshal reported to Jameson in the first place was proof enough of that fact.

Ultraa reported to Jameson also, which irritated the tall German no end.

Suddenly, he wondered just how much of a coincidence it was that he had run into Ultraa on his return trip from Shang Hai. Could Jameson have learned of the hit on Washburn and somehow know that he had taken the assignment? Koenig did not see how such a thing could have happened. Only two people knew of his involvement with the Washburn hit; himself and Lennie.

Lennie was a weasel, but he was also a professional. Koenig could not believe that the little runt had sold him out. So, if his involvement had not been discovered, then what was Washburn doing meeting with Jameson?

He needed to find out what was going on before pulling the trigger.

Koenig scouted the restaurant. In addition to the main entrance out front, there was a service entrance through the kitchen and another door discretely positioned around the far side. Most likely this was used for those moments when one of the eateries famous guests had to make a speedy withdrawal without catching the attention of the small band of paparazzi that maintained a vigil outside the famous restaurant.

That was his ticket inside.

The door was locked, of course, and fitted with an electronic keycard sensor. Koenig smiled at the arrogance of those who believed that something as small as a sensor pad could keep out someone who truly wanted in.

Koenig touched the sensor with the palm of his hand and a spark of electricity ran from his hand directly into the mechanism, shorting it with ease. Once the sensor was offline, the door lock detached and the door popped opened a crack.

Koenig smiled.

Damn I'm good.

Slipping inside was easy enough. The door was under surveillance by a camera, but that was not much of a threat against a man who could move as fast as Blitzkreig. If and when anyone checked the recording from the camera all they would see was an out of focus blur moving past the camera. There was no way the footage would ever tie him to Washburn.

At the end of the hallway was the kitchen.

Koenig took in the sweet-smelling aromas as he waited to make his move. Whatever was on the chef's special that night smelled mighty delicious. Unfortunately, it also served to remind Koenig that he had missed dinner while waiting for his mark to arrive. He covered his stomach with a hand when it began to rumble.

Once the coast was clear Koenig slipped into the restaurant proper. He made a left and circled around the wall that separated the dining floor from the washrooms. He paused at a seating section where two comfortable high-backed chairs flanked a small table with a lamp midway down the makeshift corridor and knelt down to tie his shoes, which had no laces. There was a place to sit comfortably out of sight while waiting on a table or for one's companion to emerge from the bathroom.

Reaching out with his power, Koenig brushed a finger against the electrical outlet where the table lamp was plugged in. A familiar sensation prickled his nerves as thin tendrils of electrical current passed through the lines inside the wall. It took a moment to find the right table, but finally he picked up Jameson's familiar voice.

Koenig took a seat in one of the chairs. It would look suspicious to spend more than a brief moment fiddling with his shoes. His arm draped nonchalantly over the side of the chair, Koenig listened to the conversation happening on the other side of the wall.

The voices carried along the static electrical current. It was like listening to an antique radio with really bad reception while sitting inside a hollowed-out steel barrel. Eventually, he was able to fine tune the frequency and make out what the two men were saying.

Jameson was mentioning something about how Washburn was messing up everything. He was going to ruin a lot of carefully laid plans.

"Plans made by some very powerful people," Jameson added, the unspoken threat obvious in his tone.

"It doesn't matter, Washburn said.

"Oh, but it does, Senator."

"No. It doesn't. You see, I know a few powerful people myself, Mr. Jameson. And I know about you as well. Your threats do not scare me."

"I do not make threats, Senator. I assure you."

"Then you and I have nothing further to discuss."

"You have not heard the last of this."

"Somehow, I think I have. Good day, Mr. Jameson."

"Senator Washburn."

And then Jameson was gone.

Koenig could scarcely believe what he had heard. While there was no love lost between himself and Jameson, never before had he witnessed the man back down so readily. Like the Field Marshal, Koenig suspected that Jameson was playing all sides in the hopes of coming out on top of the winning side, whichever side that might be. The Field Marshal planned to be on that winning side as well.

On that day, Koenig hoped that the honor of snuffing out Jameson's life fell to him.

But that was another day.

Now he had work to do.

Koenig broke the connection to the outlet and the light on the table brightened slightly. He smiled at a silent, private joke before walking back toward the dining area. From the corner he saw Jameson walk out of the room, his security detail falling into step once the DOD official was outside the restaurant.

Jameson climbed into his waiting car.

Koenig resisted the urge to wave as the car drove past the window.

Before he could take a step in Washburn's direction, another man sat down across from the man.

Popular guy, Koenig thought before returning to the waiting area to listen in.

4.

Karl Koenig hated conspiracies.

Unfortunately for him it was apparent that he had inadvertently stepped smack dab into the middle of one. Although he did not know what kind of influence the rotund Senator from the South wielded, he was beginning to see that it was considerable.

Washburn's second visitor of the evening worked for the White House. Although he never indicated that anyone within the upper echelon of power knew that he was meeting with the Senator, Koenig knew how to read between the lines.

Despite the duplicitous games being played just miles from the Oval Office, Koenig had the feeling that taking out the Senator was more than just a simple assignment.

It was a necessity.

The more he heard the more Koenig realized that Senator Washburn posed a clear and present threat to the Field Marshal's goals. Even though Koenig was not privy to every detail of the Field Marshal's intricate plots, he knew the man well enough to know what was and was not in the best interest of whatever plans he had brewing.

It was half an hour after the man from the White House departed that the Senator finished his dinner. The wonderful smells emanating from the kitchen only drove home the fact that Koenig had not eaten anything since earlier that morning.

He was actually pleased when the Senator decided to leave the restaurant and return to his hotel.

He needed to be away from that glorious smell.

He could eat once his task was completed.

Soon, he told his grumbling stomach.

Soon.

A security detail stayed with him the entire trip.

When Senator Washburn finally reached his hotel one of the armed men checked the room to make sure everything was in order. Once he pronounced the room was clean the Senator entered without question. He had been surrounded by armed security personnel his entire professional career.

He was accustomed to having protection.

And had grown complacent in that perceived safety.

The men and women assigned to him were very good at their jobs.

When he was finally alone he loosened his tie and let out a deep, cleansing breath. He untucked his shirt from his trousers, unbuttoning his shirt as he made his way toward the bathroom.

He opened the door and jerked.

There was a man sitting there.

"Hallo," the man said, his thick German accent easily distinguished.

"Who the hell are you?"

"Now, now, Senator," the stranger said as he stood and began pulling off one of his black gloves. "Surely, you do not think my telling you that would do you any good, do you?"

"What do you want?"

The stranger, clad all in black, smiled at that as he circled the small room like a wild, predatory cat sizing up its next meal.

"The time for stupid questions has passed as well," he answered, clearly amused.

"I don't…"

"No. Somehow I suspect you do not," the intruder said. "Tell me, Senator, does it ever bother you? Playing both sides against one another, I mean. Does that ever tug and your moral center?"

"I…" Washburn started.

The intruder held up a hand to silence him.

"Rhetorical question. No need to answer."

"What are you going to do?"

"See, now that was a good question."

"You're here to kill me, aren't you?"

The intruder stopped walking and stared at him. A smile played at the corner of his lips.

"Yes."

"Oh God!"

"Spare me, Senator."

"I can pay you."

"What need do I have for your money?"

"Are you kidding? Everybody needs money."

An uneasy smile fell across the Senator's face.

"And I have lots of it. Name your price."

"Ten million," the man said matter of fact, as if he had been biding his time until the subject of money came up.

"T… ten…"

"You asked."

"No. No. Ten million is doable. Of course, I don't have that much on me at any one time, but I can easily get it for you."

"And all I have to do is…"

"Just let me go," the Senator said, his voice excited.

"Just let you go."

"Yes."

"How do I know I can trust you?"

"You have my word."

The intruder stretched out his ungloved hand.

"Shall we, as you American's say, shake on it?"

The Senator laughed.

"Of course," he said as he reached out to take the man's open hand.

As their palms made contact the Senator stiffened as several thousand volts of electrical energy poured into his body. His eyes rolled back in his head as the convulsions started. Spittle flew from his mouth, followed by blood as he bit his tongue. After a minute of exposure, he went into cardiac arrest.

At a minute and a half his heart exploded.

Blitzkrieg broke contact and let gravity drag the lifeless body of Senator Kenneth Washburn to the floor.

The security detail was good, Blitzkrieg had to admit.

They were in the room seconds after hearing their charge's lifeless body hit the floor. First came the concerned knock at the door. When there was no answer from inside the suite, the detail broke down the door.

Guns drawn, they poured into the suite.

The Senator was alone in the room, face down on the floor.

He was not moving.

The only movement in the room came from the curtains leading to the balcony, thanks to the late-night breeze rushing in from outside.

Blitzkrieg watched from the roof of the hotel across the street as the security detail desperately tried CPR, frantically called for an ambulance, and eventually surrendered to the inevitable.

He flipped open his cell phone and dialed the number he had memorized sitting at the Open Bar a few evenings before.

"Yeah," the person on the other end answered.

"It's done."

"Never doubted you for a minute, B. You let me know the next time you get the itch."

"Lebewohl," Karl Koenig said as he flipped the phone closed.

And then he was gone. Only a blast of air marked his passing.

5.

KARL KOENIG WAS HAVING A BAD DAY.

After his meeting with the Senator he returned to the same fancy restaurant and ordered a large, almost glutinous, meal. Never had a meal tasted as sweet. After complimenting the chef on a fantastic meal well prepared, he went home and promptly collapsed into bed.

He had the most peaceful night's sleep he'd had in weeks.

The dreams were even nicer.

He stood on a great battlefield, littered with the bodies of his enemies. All of them were dead, of course. He had slain each and every one of them with his bare hands in a show of strength the likes of which no world - not this one nor the Earth where he had been born - had ever seen.

The battle had been fierce, but he had reveled in every moment of it.

Especially pleasant was the death of Jameson, whose lifeless corpse laid before him, the coward's blood in puddles around Blitzkrieg's feet.

Next to him lay Esro Brachis. His neck was broken, his head twisted around backward as if he were little more than a rag doll without a spine. Much the same way Koenig regarded the man in the waking world.

But the real thrill of his dream was Ultraa.

The same Ultraa to whom the inhabitants of this world cried out to when they needed a hero. The same Ultraa who now begged for his life in Blitzkrieg's firm grip. This was no hero. This was a sad, pathetic wretch of a man. He did not deserve the adulation of the throng.

He deserved only their pity.

The sound of his enemy's neck snapping was the greatest sound he had ever heard.

So loud was the sound that it woke him.

Fully awake, he crawled from the bed, ready for a new day. After his morning workout, Koenig shaved, showered, and dressed quickly, whistling a happy tune the entire time. It had been far too long since he had been in so wonderful a mood.

He should have known it would not last.

He sensed the Field Marshal's ill-tempered mood the moment he stepped into the man's office. The Field Marshal did not take defeat well. He also was not very good at handling rejection, failure, or setbacks of any kind very well, but Koenig allowed the man his faults. They had worked together a long time and he understood his friend's often unpredictable mood swings.

"Have you seen today's newspaper, Karl?" he asked as he slammed the folded paper in question down on the desk. A coffee cup emblazoned with the seal of The President of the United States on the side toppled under the impact, spilling an assortment of colored ink pens across the desk.

"I have not," Koenig said simply.

The Field Marshal passed the paper over and Koenig accepted it with a nod.

He read it in silence.

"Did you know him, this Senator Washburn?" Koenig asked cautiously, a lump the size of a softball growing in his throat.

The Field Marshal stopped pacing like a caged bear and faced Koenig for the first time since he entered.

"Did I know him?"

"Yes."

"Tell me, Karl. Do you know anything about this?"

"No, sir," he lied. Taking off book assignments was not permissible, although a small part of him wanted to tell the Field Marshal what he had done. He was certain the Field Marshal would thank him for his efforts. Senator Washburn's actions did not support their work.

Koenig opened his mouth to confess all when the Field Marshal started speaking. Proper etiquette required that he not interrupt his superior officer so he waited.

"This man was in town to evaluate Project Three Twelve Omega."

"What's that?" Koenig asked. This was the second time he had heard the term but he still had no clear understanding of what the project was all about. He hoped the Field Marshal would explain it.

He did not.

"What it is no longer matters. Washburn's death has caused a stir. All of the projects under his umbrella are being reevaluated even as the Secret Service investigates his death."

"The newspaper claims he died of heart failure."

"Do not believe everything you read, my friend. Especially not in an American newspaper. No. This man was murdered."

"How does this affect our operation?"

"The Field Marshal finally sat down behind his desk. He had a worried look on his face.

On the face of it, not much. Our operations will be scrutinized, but I expected nothing less and have prepared for that contingency. Everything is above board. The Secret Service will find nothing here that links this office to Project Three Twelve Omega."

"This project is one of ours?"

"Yes," the Field Marshal admitted after a moment of silence.

"I am sorry."

"So am I, Karl. Project Three Twelve Omega would have escalated my timetable. It would have put an end to all those who opposed us."

"How?"

"That is also unimportant, Karl. What should be important to you is your new assignment."

"I live to serve."

"Kenneth Washburn was a friend of this department. His death will not go unpunished. You have the task of finding his killer and bringing him or her to justice."

"But I…"

"Get out of here, Karl. Go. Bring me back the killer's head."

"Yes, sir."

"Preferably on a platter."

Karl Koenig stepped out into the crisp autumn evening.

He barely felt the cold or the sting of the driving wind. Another kind of cold had taken hold of him from someplace far, far deeper.

"What have I done?" he asked himself as he stood on the steps.

Koenig was not a man who normally brooded over decisions. He had made this one and he would deal with the consequences. He no longer had the desire to confess his involvement in the Washburn assassination, however. The Field Marshal would flay him alive if the word leaked out.

He knew what he had to do.

Someone would have to take the fall.

And suddenly, like a puzzle finally falling into place, he had just the right patsy in mind. He smiled at the thought.

Perfect! Why did I not see it before? he wondered with a perverse sense of satisfaction.

Karl Koenig flipped up the collar on his coat and stepped onto the sidewalk.

Under the shadow of the Washington Memorial, Blitzkrieg sauntered off into the setting dusk, making plans.

I wonder what ol' Heironymous is up to?

GYPSY
A SUPERHERO STORY

I CANNOT BELIEVE THEY'RE LAUGHING AT ME!

My name is Carlise Antonio and I could scarcely believe my ears. These jerks were actually laughing at me. Making jokes at my expense. Poking fun. Cat-calls even! *This is absurd,* was all I could think. *This simply isn't the way things are done.*

"I'll not tell you again," I warned them. I'm not really sure that was convincing enough though, because if I could hear the crack in my voice, then surely they could also. It's all I was able to do to fight back the tears welling up inside. This really wasn't going as planned.

"You're awfully bossy, Chichita," one of them said to me. Clearly, he was unafraid of me. "Why don't you come down here and say that to my face?" he said. I could not believe it. The bad guy was taunting me. He's supposed to be scared; cowardly, superstitious lot, and all that.

"Alrighty," was the only reply that sprang to mind as I stepped off the concrete retaining wall. Luckily, the wall wasn't very tall. I'm not scared of heights, but there was a distinct possibility of breaking my fool leg doing this. Now that I had a plan, such as it was, and knew my next move I started feeling a little more confident. Still, there was just a hint of insecurity creeping in at the edges. A twinge of doubt that threatened to explode and overwhelm me.

The landing was as graceful as ever. I'd been planning that moment for the past few years. Years spent training and honing and developing. I went out there prepared. I had a plan. Even had a strategy all mapped out and everything.

One thought was screaming through my brain, *I've got to be out of my freaking mind.*

Extending to my full height, (good thing I'm tall, around 6'1" the last time I checked) I allowed a small smile to play across my face. The leathery mask covering my eyes from just above the nose to the top of my forehead was starting to itch at this point, but I somehow managed to resist the urge to scratch. Trying to act confident and powerful, all the good traits of a super hero, I strolled casually toward the men who had been laughing at me. There were four of them and they were not nice men. Not nice at all.

And I knew all about them.

With speed far faster than one would expect from someone my size, I'm sure, I hefted the man who had called me out and slammed him against the brick wall behind where he had been standing. "Now, what was that you wanted me to say to your face, buster?" I asked him.

Buster? Did I actually say that? Ugh.

The man squeaked out a noise, but I couldn't understand him. All traces of his bravado were gone. None of them were laughing anymore, were they? Oh no. I let go and he slumped to the ground with only a groan to assure his friends that he was still alive. I may be capable of it, but I'm no killer. I'll only go so far as to kick the crap out of the bad guys. No more.

That's when I turned on the other three guys, my dress billowing about, flowing around my movements just as I had always thought it would. "Now," I said sternly, "I believe you three wanted something from me as well?" Now there was some fear in their eyes. Just a trace, but it was there. And maybe just a hint of respect.

Figuring safety in numbers, the three men overcame their trepidation at seeing one of their own downed and moved into action. From the look of it, they weren't professionally trained and moved less than gracefully. They did have raw strength on their side though. Probably a result of time spent with little else to do than lift weights and knock over liquor stores, I could only assume.

They flew at me from odd angles. I didn't doubt that they could actually hurt me if they got their hands on me, so the best thing to do was stay out of their grasp.

Using the gymnastic training tricks I'd learned over the years, managing to stay one step ahead of them wasn't that much of a chore. And I'm quite graceful too, if I do say so myself. A twist, a bend, a tuck, all of these and more were expertly employed. With moves like these I could have become a prima dancer.

But I answered another calling.

Although a part of me enjoyed this little game, I had learned better than to get overconfident. There was every reason to suspect that they could get lucky and get a grip on me sooner or later. That way leads disaster, so I dispatched them as easily as I did their compadre and left them lying unconscious in the alley where they gathered regularly to do no good.

"Well, that wasn't so hard, was it boys?" I asked the four men as I made a production of dusting off my hands like I was clapping. Silence answered, but it was good kind of silence. It was populated with the echoes of their taunts and remarks. I smiled. I couldn't help it.Knowing that I had taken a stand, stood up for myself and every other teenage girl who these men preyed on.

I fished my cell phone from one of the five pockets woven into the dress. While dialing out the numbers 9 - 1 - 1, I leapt to the top of the concrete wall I had vaulted from earlier. The phone began to ring before I got there.

"911, what is your emergency?" a raspy voice asked.

"Oh, it's not an emergency anymore," I told her. I doubt I sounded very cool. I'll have to work on that.

"I beg your pardon?"

"I've taken care of it," I told her. "I need you to send a police car over to the alley across from the Pellegrin Dance Studio at the intersection of Decker and Pierpoint. There are four guys here all ready for you. I don't think they'll give you any trouble."

"Who is this?" Somehow, I knew she was going to ask me that.

"Me?" I asked, just as I had rehearsed it a few dozen times. "I'm...". I started to answer right away. As I said, I had worked on the name for a while and was very proud of it. Until they laughed at me when I told them who I was.

"Miss?

"Uh, yeah. My name.... My, uh, that is, I'm the Gypsy." That was sooo lame. I slammed the cover shut on the phone, severing the connection. It pleased me that the 911 Operator had not laughed like those boneheads had.

As I made my way home I replayed the events of the night in my mind. I just couldn't get over how well it went once I got over my nervousness. They had laughed when I told them to, *"Step away or face the wrath of The Gypsy!"* They had laughed! How dare they!?! I wanted to explode. At that moment I wanted to shout to the world that The Gypsy was not a laughing matter. That she had the potential to be good.

To be a hero.

Not a laughing stock.

Never a laughing stock.

Then I really thought about it. Really let it all sink in. The Gypsy? What was I thinking? Maybe I should have come up with something better. Well, it had seemed a good idea at the time. Grandmother Aurelia was always telling me stories about a band of gypsies that caravanned around the countryside and the vast adventures they had. When I hatched my master plan, the gypsy motif just seemed a natural fit. Maybe I should have given it a little more thought.

I threw together a costume from some of my own clothes and a few pieces I found at the local thrift mart. Money's not overflowing around here. And I couldn't very well ask my Dad for the money. No, he'd only want to know what I needed the money for and I can never, ever tell him about this. Not ever.

The costume actually looked nice. A bright red handkerchief to hold back my short--now what did Jill call it again? Oh yeah--my raven black hair, tied up in the back, with just a small ponytail showing. This pretty much kept the hair out of my eyes while in motion. The blouse is also red, but with little patches of white dotted across it. The dress is multicolored like the dresses in Grandmother's stories, big enough to billow around and not hamper my movements. I've also got on a pair of black skin-tight leotard pants under the dress, just in case.

The Gypsy is supposed to be a hero, the last thing I needed was to be labeled a flasher. Five pockets were sewn into the dress to hold any effects I might need. House keys, cell phone, mace, and assorted smoke bombs and such, which are just too cool and I wanted them.

All in all I was pretty happy with my first night's work. I knew The Gypsy had the makings of an excellent super hero. Only time would tell, I imagined.

Over the next few months rumors swept across the city about a new hero, a mysterious vixen called The Gypsy. She did not get the press that those other guys do, nor are there photographers pounding the pavement in search of her identity or anything like that. There had been no new super villains seeking her out to make a name for themselves the way others had in the past. The Gypsy, whoever she is, *hee hee,* seems not to care for the spotlight. And her adventures, while thrilling, were not the critical earth shattering adventures that her contemporaries seem to excel at. Nor were they the kind of adventures that sold newspapers. No, The Gypsy proved little more than an interesting mystery to some, and a slight curiosity to others.

It seemed like the more infrequent the sightings, the more popular The Gypsy seemed to become.

Which suited me just fine. The limelight wasn't for me. That's not why I got involved in this. I have a life of my own to attend to. A family. I still venture out into the world as The Gypsy whenever a problem arises that needs The Gypsy's special touch. It's not like I can just patrol the city or look for a problem to solve. I was just there when a need arose that required a special brand of justice, which was becoming less and frequent of late.

That was then. This is now. The Gypsy and I began our 'partnership' about a year ago. It's so hard to imagine that t has been that long. Where does the time go?

I was walking down the street today. On the way home from school, my books cradled in my arms. It was as if I didn't have a care in the world. I admit it, I was happy. I'd aced the surprise exam that Mrs. Henderson had sprung and I caught Jeff Williams smiling at me during fourth period. *Maybe he's finally coming around. I hope.*

I haven't really had any need to go out as The Gypsy in a few days. Between a heavy workload at school and helping out around the building, what little free time I have has been occupied. Not that this stops me from keeping an ear out for trouble, mind you. I take my responsibilities very seriously. Fortunately, there has been little for Gypsy to do of late. *It looks as if The Gypsy has done her job too well.* Which was the point, after all. The Gypsy had been created to clean up the neighborhood.

And I think I've done a good job of it too. Not that I don't care, but the Gypsy's not overly concerned with saving the world, although she would probably answer the call should it ever come down to that, although if little ol' me is all that stands between Earth and total annihilation, then the Earth is more than likely doomed.

Two young girls ran past me on the street, arguing over which one of them got to be The Gypsy and which *had* to be the crook. It took all of my willpower not to laugh, but I couldn't hide the grin that split my face from ear to ear. Who knew The Gypsy would ever become so popular.

And that's then it hit me.

How long have I been thinking of The Gypsy as "her" and not "me?" This dual identity thing is for the birds, but if you want to be a super hero... well, when in Rome. At least that's how it works in the comics. How the real guys do it is anybody's guess.

To be honest, I wasn't really paying attention to much. I was aware of the two little girls playing and knew there were other people on the sidewalk, but I was living in my personal little daydream fantasy. Sloppy. I should know better than to do that. I should have been paying more attention.

As it was I, like everyone else, could only react with a startled gasp when I heard the gunshots.

An old car, I have no idea what kind it was, just another detail I missed, came around the corner so fast I half expected it to turn over. But it didn't. There were five people in the car. Four of them were hanging out the open windows, shouting and blasting away at random. They didn't have a care for anyone or anything around them.

Especially the two little girls who were frozen with terror at the edge of the street.

Where's the Gypsy when you need her. I could not believe I thought that either. I'm The Gypsy. Me.

No time for the costume though. I ran as fast as I could, abandoning my books and bag. I needed as much speed as possible to get there in time. The girls were terrified, crying for their mother. The driver of the car never even saw them. I wonder if it would have made a difference if he had.

Probably not.

As the car bore down on them, I pumped my arms and legs for all they were worth, cursing myself for not being faster. Without breaking stride, I scooped up the girls and we skidded to a halt, a rather abrupt halt, against the garbage cans outside Mr. Harcourt's little grocery store. It was a loud, painful landing.

As the girls cried in my arms, the car and the guns were gone. They had driven away as if there was nothing to stop them. *They think they can get away with this. They think they're too tough to care about the people around here. It has to stop.* I was so furious, that was all I could think about.

"It has to stop," I said to no one in particular. That phrase has been echoed throughout the city for as long as there have been people living here. The gangs run the streets. Every one is too afraid to go outside. This kind of the thing is the reason The Gypsy was created.

And she will not let these people down again.

∞

The next morning, I try to stay awake through class. I'm only partly successful. By lunch period, I'm fried. As I pick at my steak-like entree and the lime green jell-o surprise, I listen to the gossip and small talk around me, but only just. I'm just too tired to think straight.

That's when Jeff Williams sat down next to me.

God, I'm almost too tired to flirt. That can't be natural.

"Hey," Jeff says to me. "Did you hear the news?"

"What news?" I ask. There have been so many different things going on lately, that I am having trouble keeping them straight.

"There was a Gypsy spotting last night," he says. He seems genuinely excited about The Gypsy. He thinks she is cool. In a way, he thinks I'm cool. How cool is that?

For the first time today I actually smile. I can't help it. Jeff's enthusiasm is contagious. "So where was The Gypsy spotted?" I ask him.

"Well, I hear there was a shooting over near Ridgeland Park yesterday. Hey, don't you live near there? Anyway, these guys shot up an entire neighborhood. And The Gypsy tracked them down and..."

Never the end.

MAGNUS:
THE APPRENTICE

IS THERE ANYTHING WORSE THAN BEING THE NEW KID IN SCHOOL?

Yes. Being the new kid who starts two weeks after everyone else.

That summed up Andrew Kenny's current situation. His family had moved from the only home he had ever known in Chicago, Illinois to the much smaller city of Lawrenceville, Georgia. He barely had time to say goodbye to his friends before he was whisked away from Chicago's skyscrapers and transplanted into his new rural setting. In his mind, it was analogous to moving to another planet. Everything around his new home was spread out and there were very few things within walking distance except his school and a small strip mall. The only saving grace was that there was a comic book shop in the shopping center.

Andrew's mom and dad had told him that the move was necessary because of his father's transfer, which was a great opportunity for him that they couldn't turn down. While that might have been partially true, Andrew wasn't buying it. His parents loved Chicago more than he did. It would take more than a simple career opportunity to make them pack up and leave.

He knew it was because of him.

The past year had been very rough on Andrew, and as much as he hated to admit it, he took it out on his mother and father. The fact that they hadn't shipped him off to boarding school or some other place to deal with problem kids like him was something of a minor miracle. Lord knows he would have deserved it had they chosen to go that route. He had been something of a holy terror the past year and caused his family no small amount of grief.

Looking back, he could pinpoint the exact moment his life changed.

It had started with his grandfather's funeral.

He and Andrew had been very close and spent many long hours together hiking, fishing, or just talking and enjoying one another's company. His name was Jack Magnus, but Andrew called him *Grandpa Jack* because he despised being called *grandfather* because he said he wasn't old enough for that title yet. Grandpa Jack was a brilliant storyteller who often spent hours regaling young Andrew with tales of fire breathing dragons, sword-wielding knights on horseback, vicious monsters, plotting villains, and wizards with powers and abilities far beyond those of mortal men. The stories were magical and Andrew could sit and listen to his grandfather tell those amazing tall tales all day long.

He had even once asked him why he never wrote them down in a book, but Grandpa Jack would always tell him that the stories were for him and him alone. They were not for the world at large. He made Andrew promise that the stories were a secret and not to share them with anyone, not even his parents. At the time, it had not made sense why his grandfather had made such a request, but he did as he was asked. It would not be long before he realized how dangerous it was to know this secret.

During a lengthy battle with cancer, Grandpa Jack withered away to nothing. He was frail of body, but his mind remained as sharp as ever. Andrew had been sitting with him when he died. At the funeral, he and some of his cousins served as pallbearers, hefting the coffin and carrying it from the funeral home's chapel to the hearse and then repeating the process from the hearse to the gravesite that would be his final resting place.

Andrew could not remember the last time he had cried as much as he had that day. Despite his dad's foolish suggestion that he "*man up*" and not cry, he could not keep the tears from falling. He knew that his grandfather would not have minded the tears. As he stood and listened to the preacher intone about Grandpa Jack's soul and how he had gone on to a better place and was no longer in any pain he realized that none of it mattered. They were only words. He would miss his grandfather and his mother would miss her father.

As they lowered the casket into the earth, Andrew held his mother's hand.

After the funeral, the family descended on Jack's house and picked it clean. The furniture, jewelry, clothing, and assorted knickknacks he had collected on his many travels were gone. Andrew stood in the empty den where he and his grandfather had spent many an afternoon playing chess or Monopoly while Jack told him a story he had never heard before. There seemed to be no end to the new adventures he came up with. His imagination was endless.

That's when his mother walked in dragging a small trunk.

"I think your grandfather wanted you to have this," she told Andrew.

"What makes you think that?"

She pointed at the trunk. "It's got your name on it.

Sure enough, a small envelope was tied to the handle with his name emblazoned on it. He opened the envelope and retrieved the letter that was hidden within. The letter told him how much he was loved and that the contents of the trunk were for him to use when the time was right. The letter also asked that he not share what he found within the trunk with anyone. Like the stories, this trunk was their final secret. He signed it, *Love, Grandpa.*

Andrew read the letter twice before he touched the trunk. It was locked and there was no key, but the letter had explained that as well. Andrew knew where the key was, but had been sworn to secrecy. Grandpa Jack had given it to him years earlier inside a small lunchbox with the comic strip character *Mandrake the Magician* stamped into its metal frame. It had sat hidden on a shelf in his bedroom ever since.

Later that night, alone in his room, he opened the trunk.

He did not expect what he saw inside.

The trunk was filled with papers. Some were in notebooks while others were free floating. There were several items similar to the knickknacks that Jack had kept on shelves in his den. He had referred to them as *totems* several times. These totems oftentimes played a role in the wild stories Jack told. Also inside was a small stick, a box of matches, a yo-yo, a ornately carved ring, a small coin that was slightly larger than a silver dollar coin, and a book with a well-worn moleskin cover. Although the cover was faded from multiple readings, the etching remained.

On it was inscribed the words *Spell Book.*

And Andrew's life would never be the same.

Andrew quickly discovered that the stories Grandpa Jack had told all those years were true after three people approached him a few days after Jack's funeral. There were two men, named Jasper Monk and Harrison Black, plus a woman named Charisma Jones. They all claimed to be Jack's apprentices.

"Why would my grandpa need apprentices?" Andrew asked.

From these apprentices, Andrew learned that Jack had been something of a master wizard in his youth, tasked with protecting the world at large from the forces of evil that threatened to destroy it. All of the business trips he had taken over the years had been a cover to hide his true profession. It was hard to listen to the three of them talk about his Grandpa Jack in such a familiar manner, but the more they told him the more Andrew believed them. Many of the adventures they recounted were familiar to Andrew from the stories he had heard all his life.

As fantastic as it sounded, Grandpa Jack was a wizard.

That's when they Charisma dropped the bomb on him.

She told him that he was a wizard too.

It was at that moment that Andrew's life changed. Gone was the innocent little boy who had listened to his grandfather's stories and dreamed of undertaking some adventures of his own. Jasper, Harrison, and Charisma informed Andrew that their mentor's final assignment was for them to keep him safe while they trained him how to harness his powers. They were his advisors, his trainers, and his protectors.

"There are a lot of people out there that will be looking for you," Jasper told him.

"What kind of people?"

"Bad people," Charisma said softly.

As it turned out "*bad people*" was something of an understatement. During his career, Grandpa Jack had made a few enemies and now that he was gone they were coming out of the woodwork. And each of them seemed to have only one thought on their minds. Revenge. One week after learning the truth from his new advisors, Andrew's school bus was forced off the road when a water main ruptured and pushed a huge metal pipe through the concrete in its path. Luckily, no one had been hurt. His new protectors swooped in to take care of the man who was after Andrew, but he knew that there would be others.

He wasn't wrong.

The next six months consisted of one danger after another. Andrew's powers grew and his knowledge of ancient magic improved daily under his advisors' coaching. Soon he was able to protect himself, but by then the damage was done. The school had labeled him a troublemaker and threatened to suspend Andrew if things did not settle down. The news made his parents, especially his father, angry. They demanded an explanation, but Andrew was bound by his promise and his silence only widened the gulf that had grown between them since Grandpa Jack's death.

The final straw came just a month earlier when he had been attacked while in the auditorium. The man called himself Kurza and he commanded fire elementals, which he hurled at Andrew. In the course of defending himself, the auditorium was burnt to the ground. If not for quick thinking on Andrew's part the entire school would have been lost.

Unfortunately, no one else saw it that way.

Not the school.

Not the fire marshal.

And definitely not his parents.

The news of his dad's transfer came three days later.

Andrew hated starting over.

The first class at his new school was math, which was not his favorite subject. The principal walked him to the room where class had already started and introduced him to the teacher and the class. The teacher pointed him to an empty seat near the back of the room and continued her lesson. He was now officially a high school freshman. The thought scared him more than the idea of facing down a horde of angry fire demons.

Andrew's sister, Kim, was also starting classes at the same school, but she was a junior. The move had been hardest on her because she was two years from graduating and did not want to move away from all of her friends. Their mom's promise that they would each make new friends here rang hollow for both of them.

Surprisingly, Andrew's relationship with his sister remained solid. Despite everything that had happened, she did not blame him and remained cordial to him. Well, at least as cordial as a sister could be to her baby brother.

He went through the day trying to stay as invisible as possible. The events of the past six months had taught him to be careful of strangers. The irony of it all was that he now lived in a state full of strangers. He was leery of everyone and did not go out of his way to meet his new classmates. That did not stop some of the friendlier students from introducing themselves to him. He met several nice people and even found himself relaxing a bit. Perhaps his mother had been right. Perhaps he might make friends after all.

The rest of his day went pretty much the same. He started each class as an outsider who was behind the class. In most instances, he was able to catch up, but there were some homework assignments he would have to play catch up on. However, it was in his last class of the day that Andrew got his biggest surprise.

As he stepped into his American History and Civics class and almost choked on his tongue. Standing next to the chalkboard was Harrison Black, his new teacher. He overheard some of the students talking. Mr. Black was a new arrival at the school after the surprise resignation of the teacher who used to teach the class. The rumors behind the teacher's departure varied from the simple *"I heard she was sick"* to the absurd *"I heard she won the lottery and ran off to the Caribbean."* Andrew was fairly certain that his advisors had something to do with it, but of course he couldn't tell his classmates that.

After class was dismissed, Andrew stayed behind to ask Mr. Black a question about the homework assignment. Once they were alone, he dropped all pretenses. "What are you doing here, Harrison?" he asked.

"What do you think, kid?" Harrison answered. "My job is to keep you safe and I take my job seriously." He saw the look on Andrew's face. "What? Did you think moving to a new city meant it was over?"

"I was kind of hoping."

"Come on, kid. You aren't that naïve. Oh, and in class, please call me Mr. Black, okay?"

"Okay. So, what happens next?"

"Next," Harrison said with a smile, "we resume your training."

The next few days were a blur. Andrew's day consisted of a morning workout with his physical fitness nut dad followed by a full day of school. In addition to Mr. Black teaching class, Charisma had secured a job working in the school's office. Keeping his powers and training secret was still of the utmost importance so Andrew's evenings included his new part time job working at the comic book shop that was owned and operated by Jasper Monk. His parents were overjoyed when they heard the news that he'd found a job. It was the first time he had seen them happy in a long time so Andrew was determined to shield them both from his other life as much as possible. The last thing he wanted was a repeat of the incident in Chicago.

He had to tread more carefully.

The back room of Monk's Comics and Games became the training center where Andrew and his instructors continued to hone his control of the magical powers that were part of his birthright as well as training his body in more traditional ways. The days were long, but Andrew was determined to make it work. At night, he would come home, eat dinner, do his homework, and collapse from exhaustion, but it was worth it. It was his job to keep his family safe.

At the moment, his only real problem was staying awake during first period.

Unfortunately, bigger problems were heading his way.

Lord Lucius Maelstrom slammed his hand down on his antique desk.

The impact released an explosion of color as energy tendrils lanced from his fist in all directions. The desk shattered under the strain of so many mystical energies buffeting it simultaneously. Lord Maelstrom was not prone to outbursts of anger. He held it in, letting the pressure build and build until he was ready to burst. When he did let loose his frustrations his servants knew it was time to buy new furniture.

Lord Lucius Maelstrom was not really royalty. In fact, his birth name was not Lucius Maelstrom. He had fabricated his entire identity from the time his gifts first manifest themselves when he was twelve years old. The child he had been was discarded and Lucius Maelstrom took his place. He eventually came under the tutelage of a master magician who called himself Master Paragon, also not his given name. After a short time spent in Paragon's care, Maelstrom added the illustrious title of Lord to his moniker.

Lord Maelstrom eventually succeeded his teacher and took control of the family business after Master Paragon's death. There were many that believed that Maelstrom had hastened his ascension by killing his former master, but there was no proof of that, only conjecture and rumor.

Despite a less-than-stable world economy, business was booming.

Like so many others, Maelstrom's greatest defeat came at the hands of Jack Magnus. Magnus was a powerful wizard and he had placed barriers in place that hampered Maelstrom and other like him from achieving many of their goals. When he had heard that the old man had died, Lord Maelstrom cackled with joy like some comic book super villain.

"With Magnus out of the way we can finally move forward with the transfer," he had shouted to the rooftops. After years of waiting, he would finally complete a journey he had started years before.

Unfortunately, breaking down Magnus' mystic barriers proved more difficult than he had anticipated. Lord Maelstrom's abilities were great, but even his power paled in comparison to Jack Magnus.

What he needed was the amulet that his enemy had used to lock the spell that created the barriers that kept him and his followers from leaving this dimensional plane. If he ever hoped to escape he would need that amulet.

Luckily, he had an idea of where to find it. Magnus was a sentimentalist. That was his greatest weakness and Maelstrom planned to exploit it. He had summoned his lackeys (they preferred to call themselves followers, but he didn't feel the need to quibble over such details). After relaying the information to his lackeys he sent them out into the world in search of the amulet.

"Find it," he ordered. "Find my amulet!"

Andrew Kenny slipped the necklace around his neck.

He had taken the silver dollar sized amulet from the trunk and drilled a small hole in it near the edge, just large enough to slide a small hook into. He then attached the hook to a rope necklace he had in his room. This way he could keep the powerful artifact close at hand in case of emergency. It was also a way to keep Grandpa Jack close to him.

He slipped the amulet beneath his shirt and headed out the door. A school bus passed his house, but it was such a short walk that he and his sister, Kim, decided to walk it every morning. The walk was an easy one, plus it gave them time to talk.

"So, how was your first week of school?" he asked.

"Exhausting. I'm so far behind."

"I know what you mean."

"And I'm trying out for cheerleader," she said, beaming. Kim had been a cheerleader at their last school and she always seemed to enjoy it.

"That sounds cool," he said, trying to be supportive although he had little interest in sports. Like most fifteen year-old boys he did, however, have a growing fondness for cheerleaders. If his sister joined the team, it meant he might get to meet some of them.

The school day went much as Andrew expected. Nothing surprising leapt out at him from a locker or shadow. Perhaps his advisors had been wrong and no one was coming after him anymore.

At least that's what he wanted to believe.

It was his afterschool activities that Andrew enjoyed the most. His advisors were excellent instructors.

Jasper Monk was a master of several Earth born martial arts. He was teaching him some self-defense moves to start, but promised that offensive training would begin soon. Jasper demonstrated that a melding of wizardry and martial arts could be used very effectively together. His favorite defense was a spell he called the force blast. It was non-lethal, but decidedly effective. After seeing Monk in action, Andrew was more excited than ever for training.

Harrison Black was first and foremost a scholar. As Andrew had witnessed firsthand in class every afternoon, he was quite knowledgeable on a multitude of subjects. Most importantly, he was patient with his students. Andrew began to understand where the magic came from, not just how to use it. Harrison explained that knowing how something works was as important as knowing how to use it.

If Jasper honed the body and Harrison trained the mind, then Charisma was the protector of the soul. She kept Andrew grounded to reality even when his other studies strayed as far away from the realm of normality as humanly possible. She reminded Andrew what it was to be a human being. His powers had the potential for destruction and the more his skills developed the greater the possibility became. They had already witnessed it with the destruction of the school auditorium in Chicago. Without a balance of skill, training, and heart, there was a possibility it could happen again. None of them wanted that.

On Saturday's he worked at the comic book shop during the day so he could have his evenings free. His advisors understood that he was a teenager and still needed time to be a kid. After his Saturday morning workouts, the weekends were his to enjoy.

He walked out of the comic shop and squinted at the bright sun shining overhead. He had heard that it was warmer in Georgia in the fall than what he was used to in Illinois, but it was taking some getting used to. With temperatures in the mid-seventies, it was nice to get out and enjoy it. There would probably be snowing in Chicago soon. He understood they didn't get much snow in the south.

He walked down the sidewalk toward the fast food restaurant at the end of the shopping center. Charisma made them eat healthy most of the time, but the boys had started ganging up on her on Saturdays and vetoed her lunch suggestions in favor of a greasy hamburger with all the trimmings, salty French Fries, and a sugary soda. After the first two-weeks she gave up protesting and enjoyed a day of gluttony.

The restaurant was crowded and he recognized some of the locals that worked in the strip mall and some that he went to school with. Sitting in a corner booth was his sister and some of her new cheerleading friends. Kim had been accepted onto the squad the week before and was enjoying hanging out with her new friends. Andrew thought about going over to say hello, but decided against it. The last think Kim needed was her dorky little brother embarrassing her in front of her friends.

As he stood in line a strange feeling made the hair on his neck stand up. It was an uneasy feeling that told him something was wrong. He just didn't know what. That's when he saw them enter. There were three of them. They were large men with tattoos running the length of their muscled arms. They took their place in the line next to Andrew's, but only two of them remained together. The third got into line behind Andrew.

He didn't recognize them, but Andrew could feel a mystic energy emanating from them. He had felt such waves before, but never as primal. It felt like waves of raw power buffeting him from each of them and then aftershocks as the waves bounced off one another like ripples in a pond. He had felt something similar before when he faced Kurza back in Chicago. Whoever these men were, they were powerful wizards, but unfocused.

If they were here for him, and he couldn't imagine it was just a coincidence that they had walked into this restaurant at the same time he had, then things could get ugly rather quickly. He had to get away from all of these people. If they made a move here, then they could get hurt. His sister could be hurt.

Casually, Andrew stepped out of line and walked toward the exit.

The man in line behind him followed and grabbed him by the shoulder just as Andrew reached the exit. "And just where do you think you're going?" he snarled.

Andrew swallowed hard. The last thing he wanted to do was fight this guy and his friends. People might get hurt. Plus, with three to one odds he wasn't so sure he could take them. His training was good, but he was not ready to deal with these odds yet.

He stared up at the man who towered over him.

"Who sent you?" Andrew asked, trying to keep the fear from his voice.

The big man laughed, but before he could say anything else his friends walked over to them. "Why don't we take this outside?" one of them said softly.

"My thoughts exactly," Andrew said as he pushed open the door.

As soon as he felt the warm sun on his face, Andrew ran.

The big guys gave chase, but the teenager had speed and stamina on them. He quickly widened the gap between them as he leapt over the retaining wall that separated the restaurant from the shopping center.

When he hit the asphalt, Andrew was already moving. He ran around the back of the shopping center. The last thing he wanted was for anyone to get hurt so he made for the closest place he could think of that was empty. Plus, he hoped to get help through the rear entrance of the comic shop. He just hoped Charisma and Harrison were still in the back.

The back of the shopping center was a maze of stacked pallets, dumpsters, empty boxes, and assorted junk that just happened to end up there. Jasper had set up some training exercises back there. At the time, Andrew hated it. Not only was it filthy out there, but it smelled. But now, he was happy for it.

Andrew ducked behind a stack of broken pallets from the sporting goods store. The broken pieces of wood gave him adequate cover, but still allowed him to keep an eye on his pursuers. The three men slowed as they rounded the corner. They had lost sight of him and didn't know where he was. All they knew was that he was close.

They split up. One of the bruisers went around, hoping to come in from the retaining wall that ran the length of the mall. The wall was twenty feet tall and not easily accessible from the other side, but Andrew knew better than to underestimate his foes.

"With my luck these guys can fly," he mumbled.

The other two began moving deeper onto the cracked concrete, but they were careful, walking slowly and checking each potential hiding place for him. It would slow them down, but eventually they would find him. He contemplated making a break for the rear entrance of Monk's shop, but the door was probably locked. Something told him he'd never make it before these guys caught him.

He needed to think of something fast.

One of the first spells he had learned was called *distraction*. It had come in handy in Chicago when Kurza and his goons had come for him. He hoped it would work against these guys as well. He concentrated, his eyes focusing on an area behind them as he mouthed the words to the spell.

A crashing noise made both men turn simultaneously. It had worked. The young wizard had sent a distracting noise directly into both of their minds. For all of their raw power, neither of them appeared to be the brains of the operation. They obviously worked for someone, but he had no idea whom it could be. He had inherited quite a few enemies from Grandpa Jack and they just kept coming out of the woodwork. And there were some he had not yet met.

The men doubled back and looked for the source of the noise they heard. There was nothing there, obviously, but with their backs turned, Andrew made a break for the door to the comic shop. He was about halfway there when he heard a shout from behind him.

"He's over there!"

Andrew had forgotten about the third man who was standing on the twenty-foot wall at the back of the property. Somehow, he had managed to reach the top. From his perch, he had a perfect view of the entire lot.

His shout had alerted the other two and they bore down on Andrew, who no longer had any place to hide. Andrew made fists and pointed them at the two men.

They slowed; wondering what he was up to.

Andrew smiled as a soft blue glow formed around his white-knuckled fists. He mouthed the words, "force blast" around a wide cocky grin--

--Then spun and aimed the blue force blasts at the man on the wall. The blasts hit him square in the chest and head and knocked him off the wall. He dropped twenty feet and landed out of sight with a loud crash on the other side of the concrete wall.

Andrew spun on his heel as he had been taught and aimed his glowing fists at the two men advancing on him.

Having witnessed their friend being dispatched so quickly, they slowed.

"Just hand over the amulet, kid," one of them said. His voice was like a growl.

"What are you talking about?"

"Don't play stupid kid. Just hand it over and this ends."

"Yeah. Right."

The men had been putting space between them as they talked. It was a classic move that Andrew remembered from Harris's history lessons. By splitting his focus, if the young magician attacked one then the other could swoop in and catch him off guard. It was a sound plan and would probably have worked if he hadn't been trained against such a ploy.

The one on the right lunged and Andrew threw the force blast at the one on the left even as he twisted his body against the approaching attacker. The stranger came in wide and his swing missed its target.

Andrew grabbed his arm and used the man's momentum against him, throwing him easily in the direction of the comic shop. Once his opponent was off balance and no longer touching ground Andrew hit him with a double force blast that propelled him toward the rear of the shop.

He hit the wall with enough force to shatter the door inward.

Andrew spun back toward the remaining man. The plan had been to get a bead on him and drop him with another force blast before he knew what hit him. Unfortunately, the man was faster than Andrew expected.

The large bruiser tackled the teen and knocked him to the concrete. The impact expelled the air from his lungs and Andrew gasped for breath as the big man grabbed at his shirt. The amulet fell from its hiding place and dangled from the string.

The man smiled as he tore the string from the young magician's neck. "I believe this is what I'm looking for," he sneered into the boy's ear.

"Give that back," Andrew said angrily.

The man laughed.

"You heard the man," a new voice said from nearby.

Andrew immediately recognized the owner of the voice, but it was the last person he ever expected.

Andrew's sister stood at the entrance, her hands on her hips and a scowl on her face. He had seen this look before. She was not happy. "I believe you should let him go now," Kim said, her voice never changing tempo.

"And just who do you think you are, little girl?"

"His sister."

"Aw, ain't that sweet?" the bruiser barked. "I've got business with your baby bro here so you should shove off before I decide to have business with you."

"That's not a very smart idea," Kim said as her eyes began to glow. Apparently, Andrew wasn't the only one with a secret. "We won't like that."

"Oh yeah. Who's we? You got an army in your pocket?"

Kim smiled. "Not exactly. They're behind you."

"Do I look stupid enough to fall for that?"

"Don't make me answer that," someone said from behind him.

The bruiser turned and saw Harrison, Jasper, and Charisma. Harrison had the man Andrew tossed through the door held immobile against the wall. The bruiser was outnumbered, but they had to wonder if he was smart enough to realize it.

He was. The man released his grip on Andrew.

Andrew snatched the necklace back and held it firm.

"Why don't we have a little chat," Jasper said as he approached the bruiser. The big man sighed. He had lost the day.

An hour later they were all sitting around the table in the training room.

After interrogating the men, Jasper had let them go with the knowledge that if they were ever seen around here again it would not end so nicely for them. Jasper explained that the men told him they worked for Lord Lucius

Maelstrom, which meant nothing to Andrew or Kim. Neither of them had ever heard of him.

Andrew was more interested in what had happened with his sister. "So, what was that out there?" he asked. "With the eyes?"

"Oh, what," Kim said playfully. "Did you think you were the only one Grandpa Jack told his stories to?"

"You mean you're…"

Kim shrugged.

"And all this time you knew about me and never said anything?"

"It was a secret. Grandpa Jack asked me to keep an eye on you. He said you were special. He taught me a few things to help me out."

"I'll say," Charisma added. "That bit with the glowing eyes was effective."

"Just a parlor trick. Nothing more than for show, I'm afraid. Now, that force blast thing you did, that was way cool."

"Yeah. It was, wasn't it?" Andrew said proudly.

"Maybe you can teach me?"

Jasper smiled. "I think we can fit you in."

"Yes!" Kim shouted.

"Well, she is a Magnus," Charisma joked.

"No doubt about it," Harrison added.

"So, when do we start?"

Lord Lucius Maelstrom was not happy.

Not only had his lackeys failed him, but had also told the boy's protectors about him. No doubt they would be on guard now. The one good thing to come from this debacle was that he now had definitive proof as to the amulet's whereabouts. All he had to do was come up with a plan to take it.

"Well, Magnus," he said. "Looks like our game's not done after all."

BEYOND THE HORIZON

KELVAN STARED OUT AT THE HORIZON AND FELT THE KNOT IN HIS STOMACH tighten.

It was not a new sensation. The knot first made its presence felt the day after he made his decision and it had continued to grow tighter and tighter as the moment approached. In fact, he was beginning to doubt the feeling would be going away any time soon. At first, he had thought it was a sign from the gods that he was making a tragic mistake, but he quickly dismissed that notion as folly. He had felt a similar tightening in his gut when he decided to pursue the lovely raven-haired Leela and that had turned out to be one of the greatest choices of his life.

No, he was certain that his decision was the right one. As he stared out at the horizon, watching as the fiery red and orange remnants of the sun retreated once again to its place of slumber somewhere beyond the mountains to the west, past the point of what was known, he realized that he was right. In that moment, there was no uncertainty, no second-guesses, and no remorse. Only a small knot of fear remained, but it was not enough to deter him.

The decision was made.

There would be no turning back.

Come morning, before the sun rose over the smaller mountains that encircled the valley he called home, he would be gone. He had written a farewell letter to his family and friends and planned to leave the parchment on the family table where he knew it would be discovered when his mother began preparations for the morning meal. By the time his family knew of his plan it would be too late to stop him.

As the final flicker of light disappeared, Kelvan felt tiny hands tug at him from behind. "Time to eat," he heard his youngest sister, Kara, tell him in that sing-song way she had that made every word out of her mouth sound like laughter. "Come now! Now!" He was surprised that she had been able to approach without his hearing her. Her favorite pastime was to come up behind people as silently as possible and startle them. Most of the time she was unsuccessful, but she was getting better at it. Their mother now expected Kara to jump out at her from every shadow after an early morning surprise several days prior.

Kelvan relented with a laugh and scooped his darling little sister up in his powerful hands and tickled her belly as he carried her back to the cottage they called home. Her infectious barks of giggling laughter echoed through the night, growing louder and louder.

He would miss young Kara the most.

Family meal was a tradition in Kelvan's home. Every night the entire family would gather and spend time together. As usual, Mother had cooked up a feast worthy of a land baron's mansion instead of a farmer's modest cottage. The heavy wooden table that Father's father had made with his own hands long ago was overloaded with so much food that Kelvan sometimes feared it might snap into kindling under the weight of it all. The sweet aromas of his mother's recipes mingled in the air and made the entire home smell delicious. Knowing that it might be the last meal prepared by his mother that he might ever eat, Kelvan savored every bite and even went back for seconds.

Father sat in his traditional place at the head of the table and held court over Kelvan, his mother, his three older brothers; Vena, Marn, and Kelt, and his two sisters, Vala who was older than everyone except Vena, with Kara as the youngest. Father asked each of them in turn, from the oldest to the youngest, about their day. Every one of them took their turn, including the youngest among them. Surprisingly, little Kara had some of the best stories, although she tended to take a long time getting to the point she was trying to make.

Father was an excellent listener and as each child spoke they knew they had his full, undivided attention. The three eldest boys usually had the least to say since they spent all day working the fields of the family farm with Father, but they told tales of their day just the same for the rest of the family. No doubt they spoke of things throughout the day, but somehow they made working the farm sound interesting.

Kelvan's older sister, Vala, worked as an aide to one of the matriarchs of the valley's lone village, which was just a short trip away by horse. Vala's duties for the Matriarch, whom she called Miss Ella, varied from day to day, so the family always enjoyed listening to her stories.

Today, Vala had accompanied the Matriarch into the hills where she met with the Hill People to discuss the option of building a dam to store a reservoir of water for the valley and the Hill People to use as needed. Vala was confident that negotiations were successful and that construction would begin soon. This news excited Kelvan's brothers, who were always eager to take on new challenges, especially if it bought them a small reprieve from the harsh reality of working the family farm.

Like his sister, Kelvan also worked in the village. His job, however, was nowhere near as glamorous as hers seemed to be. Kelvan served as apprentice to Devok Mahjor, the village historian. Kelvan was learning the history of the village and was assisting the historian in creating a new map of the valley, including the sections of the mountains and hills that surrounded the village.

During the past months they had traveled extensively as they mapped every path, trail, and home in the valley. It was an enormous task, but it was nearing completion. Kelvan had probably knew the valley better than even his father or his father before him.

Kelvan's studies of the valley's history had turned up some very intriguing information. Although it was commonly accepted that no one ever left the valley, and with only a handful of exceptions, no one had in several generations, Kelvan found documentation of ancient explorers who had braved the journey over the horizon to see what was out there. Unlike those who later followed in their footsteps, these explorers were hailed as brave heroes as opposed to brain-damaged heretics as they were today.

Unfortunately, none of those who had gone over the horizon had ever returned.

Those who stayed behind took this as a sign from their deities that leaving the valley was dangerous and that they were better off staying put to live out the life that had been so graciously given to them by their ever-benevolent gods. Those who left were deemed deviants and never spoken of again except as object lessons to the next wandering soul who felt the call of the unknown.

Kelvan was one such wandering soul.

After making his astonishing discovery, Kelvan had naturally told his family during evening meal. To his surprise, not only did his family dismiss the notion of leaving the valley as dangerous, but Father had commented on how foolhardy it all sounded. He said that such a thing was something only someone without a dollop of common sense would ever conceive. "I have everything I need here," he had said matter of fact. "For what reason would I ever want to leave the village?"

That night, while lying in his bed and staring at the ceiling while listening to his brothers snore, Kelvan made his decision. He would do it, if only to prove to his father that it could be done.

He was going over the mountains and beyond the horizon.
He had to know what, if anything, was out there.

Kelvan dressed quietly in the dark.

He had stared at the ceiling in the room he shared with his brothers all night. He had hoped to get some sleep, but he was too excited to begin his journey so the peace of dreaming eluded him. Adrenaline coursed through his body. He was ready to go and as the hour of his departure drew nearer, his excitement grew.

He paused at the door and took a last look at the family room. He hoped that he would be able to return home after he found that which he sought, but he understood that he may never make it back this way again.

As he closed the door behind him his only thought was that someday his family would understand why he had to leave.

With only the stars and a copy of the map he had made of the mountains to the west as his guide, Kelvan stepped off of his family's farm into the night.

The unknown awaited him.

Since he had made the decision to go, Kelvan had mapped out the path he would take in great detail. He knew the way so well he could walk it with his eyes closed. Or in the dark. He knew that if he were to use a torch then he would be spotted and possibly pursued and dragged back to face his father's disappointment. Neither of those options were particularly appealing so he moved on in the dark, slowly and carefully measuring each step and handhold as he began to climb.

The climb was difficult, but manageable. Kelvan had been climbing these rocky paths since he was able to walk. Despite traveling by starlight, he made it to the top just as the sun began its rise from behind the eastern hills behind him. He stood atop the highest rock he could find and watched as the deep purples and reds brightened until only a brilliant blue remained. The valley looked beautiful in the morning light, especially from above and Kelvan felt the first pangs of sadness for leaving.

As the farm beasts began to stir below, Kelvan turned his back on everything he had ever known and started down the mountain into the unknown.

After the fourth sunset, Kelvan was beginning to wonder if he had made a mistake. He had been walking for days and had yet to see much of anything. There were rocks and plants, grass and dirt, all things he had seen before. Disappointment began to creep in on him. He had been so certain that he would find something wonderful and exciting, but so far there was… nothing.

"How could I have been so wrong?" he mumbled.

He found a stream and made camp for the night. As he sat next to the fire and stared up at the sky above, he thought about going back and wondered what he family must think of him. He missed them, especially young Kara. If he returned, would they welcome him back with open arms? he wondered. Or would they turn him away?

The thought of it scared him. He decided he would give it just one more day. If he did not find anything by the next sundown he would turn around and go back home.

The next morning Kelvan started on the last leg of his journey. He walked with purpose. If he was going to find something he had to do it today. Despite making no discoveries, he remained convinced that there was something out there just beyond the horizon.

He knew it.

He felt it.

Kelvan prayed that he would find it.

As the sun began its downward trajectory, racing the determined young man toward the horizon, Kelvan felt his hopes begin to fade. He saw a hill ahead of him, not quite as high as those that surrounded his home valley did, but they still stretched toward the heavens. From atop there he would get a good look at the lands surrounding him. Maybe from there he could see what was out there. If he planned to follow his self-imposed deadline, he would have to hurry to reach the hills before nightfall.

He picked up the pace.

The climb was not a difficult one, but it took him longer to reach the peak than he had guessed. It was dark by the time he reached the top. Once he was there, however, he knew it was worth every ounce of sweat the climb had taken out of him for the sight he beheld made his spirit soar.

Not far away he could see the twinkling lights of a sprawling city. It was much larger than the tiny village he had called home. Kelvan was so excited that he wanted to run down the mountain, but common sense prevailed. Trying to traverse the unfamiliar in the dark was reckless at best. The smart thing to do was to wait until sun up before making the journey. He made camp.

Come morning, Kelvan was on the move.

By midday he reached the edge of the wondrous city. It stretched out before him as far as the eye could see. The dwellings were larger than those he knew, some reaching as much as three or four stories high. The streets were full of people walking and milling about, some selling their wares while others simply tried to navigate their way through the crowd. Kelvan had never before seen so many people gathered in one place before as he walked into the market. The sensation and mixture of exotic smells in the air threatened to overwhelm him.

He stopped at one of the stands that was filled with various fruits and vegetables of all sizes and colors. Most of them he recognized, but there were a few the likes of which he had never before seen. "Good day, my friend," the man working the stand said, all smiles.

"Good day to you as well," Kelvan said as he returned the smile.

The seller motioned toward the delicious display in front of him. "What looks good to you today, my good man?"

"Everything," Kelvan said as his picked up a jumjak pear and handed over a couple of coins he had brought with him.

"An excellent choice," the seller said as he took the coins and looked at them.

A look passed across the man's face that made Kelvan stop before taking a bite of his purchase. "Is something the matter?" he asked.

"What kind of currency is this?" He held it up to the light for a better look. "I've never seen anything like it."

"Oh." Kelvan's cheeks flushed red. "I'm not from here. I'm just passing through. I came from the village."

"Village?"

"Yes, sir. It's just over those mountains there," he said, pointing toward the direction he had come. "About five days walk."

"Who knew there was anything out there?"

"It's a small farming village, but it's home."

"And what brings you to our fair city?"

"Exploring," Kelvan said. "Maybe you can help me."

"Perhaps."

"Are there other cities like this one? Do you know what lies beyond the city limits?"

"Beyond the..." he said skeptically, as if he couldn't believe someone had actually asked such a ridiculous question. "How would I know what is out there?"

"Aren't you curious? Do you not travel?"

"I have everything I require right here," the seller said flatly. "For what reason would I ever need to leave the city?"

Kelvan was taken aback as the echo of his father's words was thrown back at him. He couldn't speak, didn't know what to say. So he ran. He ran and did not stop until he was well clear of the market. He had hoped that the people here would be different, but he could see that these people lacked an adventurous spirit, much the same as those in his village. It saddened him.

Kelvan spent four glorious days in the city, taking in everything he could and enjoying the exotic flavors the city had to offer. On the fifth day he knew it was time to move on so he packed his bag and headed toward the city limit to the east. He would continue walking toward the horizon. There had to be more out there for him to see. There simply had to be.

And he would find it.

Even if it took the rest of his life.

Kara stared out at the horizon and felt the knot in her stomach tighten.

It was not a new sensation. The knot first made its presence felt the day after her brother left. It had been many days since she discovered Kelvan's note on the family's meal table, but she still returned to this spot every day and scanned the horizon for some sign, some glimpse of her brother.

So far she had found none.

Although she no longer cried herself to sleep at night, Kara remained sad most of the time. Happiness returned to her life in small doses, but she knew the emptiness of Kelvan's absence would always remain with her. Her father no longer spoke of his rebellious son after condemning the boy's adventurous spirit for making his mother sad. He would never admit it aloud, but she knew Father missed Kelvan almost as much as she did.

Kara could not understand her family's attitude. She understood why her brother did what he did for she too shared his wandering soul and adventurous spirit, but she would not share that with her family.

Kara smiled as she watched the sun set beyond the horizon. She still missed

Kelvan and always would. She knew he was out there somewhere and hoped that one day they would be reunited.

Perhaps one day I'll follow him, she thought, but could never say so aloud. *And then I'll see what lies beyond the horizon.*

MOON GIRL
"BLOOD MOON"

THE FIRE BURNED BRIGHTLY.

Six robed believers circled the roaring flames, their hands held out to the sides with their bare fingers only an inch apart, but never touching one another. For the past three hours they stood still, chanting in rhythmic harmony until at last they were ready. Their most-honored leader, his face hidden in shadow beneath the hooded cowl he wore, took a step closer. He held the sacred cup, one of the most prominent relics in their order's care, above his head. The flames highlighted his strong chin. The fire was the only source of light save for the blood red full moon above that was partially shrouded by thick clouds that threatened snow.

Eyes turned heavenward, the most-sacred leader spoke. "From the void, we summon!" he started and the others chimed in, repeating his words.

The most-sacred leader turned the cup on its side and a thin river of the deepest red flowed into the flames, glowing a scarlet crimson as it reflected the flame's light back upon itself. "The blood moon marks the path!" the leader said, and his companions echoed the sentiment.

The flames erupted as if something extremely flammable had been tossed onto it. Several of the believers recoiled slightly as the fire expanded rapidly, the flames leaping out toward them, but not actually making contact.

"Heed our call and come forth!"

The leader poured the last of the ruby-red liquid into the flames and smiled as the flames morphed from yellows and orange to a more menacing crimson. He smiled. It was almost time. "In darkness, we dwell," he intoned. "In darkness, we die. We beseech the void to send us a cha…"

Before he could finish the right of supplication, a bolt of bright white lightning erupted from its hidden fortress in the sky bonfire with an ear-shattering CRACK! as it striked true at the center of the circle of flames. Unprepared for the violence of the power they have conjured, the robed believers were knocked back, thrown away from the fire with great force.

"That did not…" he started, pausing as pain shot through his body. "Did not work as… we…planned." The most-honored leader lifted himself up with hands and elbows, groaning softly until he froze in place, his gaze transfixed.

Staring wide-eyed at the last thing he had expected to see. The-- his brain couldn't form the right words to describe the creature that stood before him, but she-- and of that he was certain, it was a she-- she stood amid the flames, not quite completely here nor there. He could see right through her.

"By The Eternal!" he shouted.

She had been looking forward to a quiet evening at home.

Clare Lune's life had become a series of wild adventures over the past couple of years since learning the truth of her origins and obtaining her family's mystic Moonstone. That heirloom, once in her possession, made her all but invincible in battle. And oh, the battles there had been. Since migrating from her home in fabled Samarkand, the Princess of the Moon had faced a plethora of enemies ranging from those with arcane powers to common street criminals. It was a rough life, but a fulfilling one.

And today had been no exception.

Some clown had thought it a good idea to rob the Museum of Natural History and sell the pilfered artifacts for a hefty profit. Unfortunately, for the thief, he grabbed the wrong artifact, an ancient wand that once belonged to a sorcerer of extraordinary power. Legend has it that at the moment of his death the sorcerer placed an enchantment on the wand, a curse to any that dared tempt to possess his property. Unaware of this, the idiot thief found himself transformed into a hideous monstrosity that promptly began tearing up the city that morning.

And it had been up to Clare's alter ego, Moon Girl, to stop him.

So, like any other good superheroine worth her salt, she pulled on her tight top and short shorts with partial moon-shaped emblems on them, put on her sexy strappy high-heeled shoes that, in hindsight were not the smartest fashion choice for her occupation, and rushed headlong into danger. She was just glad it was a Saturday so she didn't have to skip out on her students.

Once the situation was under control and things were starting to return to normal, Clare slunk away from the authorities and their incessant questions with only three things on her mind. At the top of that list was a big bowl of freshly popped popcorn. Second was a quiet night in front of the TV with her favorite guilty pleasure movie. But first, what she really needed was a long, hot, steamy shower.

Clare returned to her apartment where, after a lovely pasta dinner, she showered. No matter how many times she tried, there was just no easy way to get the smell of enchanted beast out of her hair. She had just stepped out of the tub and slid the curtain closed behind her with one hand while drying her hair with a towel in the other when she felt it. It wasn't a new sensation, but one she hadn't felt in a long time.

Teleportation.

She was being summoned, but to where? She wasn't certain. Her flesh puckered as thousands of goose pimples sprang up all over her body. Her extremities tingling, Clare reached for the robe she had left hanging on the hook on the bathroom door.

Her hand passed through it as if it weren't there.

"Oh, crap," she muttered as her bathroom began to fade away around her. She hated teleportation. It always made her nauseous.

The next thing Clare knew she was surrounded by flames.

The most-honored leader couldn't believe his eyes.

He and his brothers had called upon the Spirit of the Moon to send them a champion. He assumed that, at best, the Spirit would grace them with an army of her mightiest warriors. Instead, he saw only a single, tiny girl materialize inside the flames. *Surely there must be some mistake*, he thought. *How can one girl hope to save us?*

The girl pitched forward on unsteady knees and fell out of the flame just a few feet in front of him.

And why is she naked? He couldn't help by wonder.

The leader pushed himself off the ground, his eyes never once shying away from the woman as steam rose from her body in the crisp winter chill. No matter what his ideal champion might be, the Spirit of the Moon had seen fit to send this one to save him and the others. He would not dishonor the Spirit Mother's wisdom.

"It worked!" he shouted so the others could hear. "It worked! Our summons has been answered!"

The others slowly got to their feet as well, all of them staring at the naked woman sprawled on the grass before them.

"Our champion has arrived," the most-honored leader said.

That's when their champion threw up.

Clare tried her best, but she couldn't hold it in any longer.

With a heave, she vomited and instantly regretted her dinner choice of pasta with onions and meat sauce. It had tasted so good going in, but burned coming back up. After the heaving stopped, she felt their eyes upon her. Clare looked around and saw the six robed figures watching her intently.

And then she remembered that she wasn't wearing any clothes.

"Great Luna!" she exclaimed, as she often did when things didn't go her way.

Clare scooped up the towel and wrapped it around herself as best she could, knowing it was a futile maneuver. She made a mental note to buy some larger towels as soon as she got back home from... wherever the hell she was at the moment.

Clare Lune, the Moon Girl, was clearly confused by her new surroundings. "What happened?" she asked. "One minute I'm stepping out of a nice hot shower, the next, *BOOM*, here I am." She looked around at the unfamiliar surroundings. "And speaking of which, where exactly am I anyway?"

None of the robed figures answered.

"Uh, hi. Hello," she said, once again trying to get an answer and feeling rather foolish in her current predicament. "Hi. Look, *uh*, not to seem rude or anything, but where…" she tried to motion toward her surroundings, but decided keeping her modesty covered was a better use of her hands.

One of the robed individuals approached, taking off the robe in the process. Clare was surprised to see that it was a woman. She had a kind face and friendly smile. "You honor us with your presence, Mighty One," she said with supplication as she slipped the robe around Clare's shivering shoulders. "We have called you forth to beg for your assistance. Our community stands on the brink of extinct--"

Clare held up a finger to silence her. "Um, hold that thought for a second," she said as she cinched closed the robe. Perhaps one of you could find me some real clothes?"

"Of course," the woman said and with a look one of the other robed figures ran off. A few minutes later he returned carrying an armful of clothing of various sizes and colors. Mostly they were dresses, but there was a couple of pair of men's pants as well. She selected a pair of trousers, a dark shirt that was tight around the neck. A white button up shirt over top of that completed the look. The only shoes available were old, ugly clodhoppers, but they beat running around in the cold with bare feet. The last thing she needed was to catch pneumonia.

"Much better," she said once she was dressed. It wasn't quite like the brightly-colored uniform she wore into battle with its yellow, red, and blue, but it would do. "Now what seems to be the problem?" she asked the woman who had offered her the robe.

"You are our last hope. A fortnight ago, a group of strangers came to Barrow Ridge, our village," she said, pointing to a small burning town on the not too distant horizon. Mostly all Clare could see was the glow from the fires.

"We welcomed them with open arms at first, but we soon found out they were less than they originally appeared."

"What does that mean?"

"Were-beasts," the most-honored leader added.

"I beg your pardon?"

"They are monsters," the woman said. "They are not like we."

"And these creatures have taken over your town?" Moon Girl asked.

"Yes," the leader said softly. "And they are still there."

Moon Girl pointed at one of the horses grazing nearby. It is saddled and the rein wrapped around a tree limb. "Why don't I go take a closer look at these were-creatures," she said as she mounted the horse.

"Be back soon."

Moon Girl rode her borrowed steed to the edge of town. It looked deserted, save for the assorted fires burning around the village. There were no signs of the monsters her robed abductors mentioned. Of course, she knew better than to simply dismiss their fears out of hand. After all, she herself had seen many a strange thing that defied conventional explanation.

Barrow Ridge, she thought as she slowed the horse at the edge of town. *Funny, but that name seems awfully familiar. Now where have I heard that name before? While I don't applaud their means of "summoning" me, these people are desperate for help. I'll be sure to give them a stern lecture--*

She saw movement out of the corner of her eye. These creatures, werewolf or not, knew she was there. "Just as soon as I spring this obvious trap," she said as she pulled back on the reins, her horse rearing up on its hind legs.

Moon Girl dismounted and smacked the horse's hindquarters, sending it fleeing from the danger zone. The were-creatures came out of the woodwork, materializing from the shadows like something out of a nightmare. They were large and hairy, their claws and teeth looked sharp, and they smelled faintly like wet dog.

"Hello, boys," she said calmly, even as she braced for attack.

She was not disappointed as the were-creatures leapt at her en masse, piling atop her as their claws and teeth slashed at anything that moved, including each other.

Aside from being invincible in battle, Moon Girl's heritage, amplified by the Moonstone, granted her superior strength. She used that strength to push her attackers away with violent force. Sensing her power, the werewolves hesitated a moment, uncertain what to make of the tiny creature they had considered easy prey only seconds earlier.

Once upon a time, this had been the extent of her abilities. Unfortunately for her attackers, Clare had spent the past couple years learning about the greatest warriors from her fabled homeland, Samarkand. She had discovered that there was more to being the Princess of the Moon than she had ever suspected.

Now that she had bought herself a second to concentrate, Moon Girl felt a familiar tingle rise within her as the sphere of energy grew inside her. She could feel the energizing sensation fill every pore, fill every extremity of her being. This, she knew, was power.

She held her hands in front of her, palms outward toward her enemy. "You puppies need a severe whacking across the nose," she said, trying to mimic the bravado her former partner, Prince Mengu, often displayed in battle. She had observed that his well-placed barbs had the odd effect of throwing his enemies off balance. She hoped it worked as well on creatures of the night as it did on lowly criminals.

If not, well she still had the means to back it up. "Since I don't have a newspaper, a few well-placed moon beams should do the trick," she said as she unleashed a Moon Beam from each hand, sending a lance of pure energy toward a nearby beasties that were ready to pounce. The brilliant blue and white beam hit its target and sent it crashing through the wall of a nearby building, one of the few that was not on fire.

That got their attention. The creatures took a tentative step back, shocked by the young human's abilities. They were not used to having their prey fight back with such severity.

"Does no one enforce the leash law around here?" Moon Girl said playfully as her fingers danced around wildly, silently readying one of the earliest tricks she had learned. Creating a containment spell out of the same blue-white energy, Moon Girl wrapped up the creatures and pinned them against a nearby wall.

"Let's see you break out of these moon bands, pups," she said once they were secured. Of course, the creatures struggled against the bonds, flexing their powerful muscles in an attempt to break free. Their guttural growls grew louder and louder until Moon Girl began to wonder if they might actually manage to break free.

"Persistent little were-beasts, aren't you?" she said, trying to calm the down the way one might talk down an angry pet Rottweiler. She couldn't risk letting them loose again because they were dangerous. If there was even the slightest possibility they could break the holding bands then she needed to do something fast.

Moon Girl stood her ground in front of the creatures. Their rage was focused directly on her, each one staring directly at her, which was exactly what she had wanted.

"Sleep," she whispered while, with an offhanded flick of her hand, as if it were nothing more than a minor annoyance, Moon Dust flew from her fingers and settled over the angry beasts.

This was an older trick, one she had picked up at an early age when babysitting the royal terror that was her cousin. What she called Moon Dust was actually particles of the same energy that powered her Moon Beams. Similar in use to pixie dust, Moon Dust was a calming agent. As it had with her bratty cousin all those years earlier, the Moon Dust worked on the creatures behind her.

They were fast asleep.

"Is it just me or did that seem way too easy?" she muttered.

Another sound caught her attention and Moon Girl turned to see the villagers returning to their homes. The six robed figures she met earlier led the way.

"She has done it!" the most-honored leader proclaimed proudly as he led the throng back into their village. "Our champion has slain the beasts!"

Moon Girl noticed that the villagers were returning home with axes, knives, and other sharp cutlery at the ready. A sudden unease fell upon her. "Not exactly," she told the leader. "They are not dead. Merely sleeping."

The leader pulled a stone, one very similar to her Moonstone, in fact, from beneath his robe. "Then we will see to it, champion," he said. "You are relea--"

"Not so fast," she said, a small flick of her finger Moon Girl created a thin band of light energy around the leader's mouth that stopped him in mid-sentence before he could reverse whatever mystic juju had brought her there and send her away. She had many questions and was not planning to leave until they had been answered to her satisfaction.

"I have a couple of questions," she said.

"Do you indeed?" another robed man asked as he raised his axe to make sure she could see it. There was no disguising the threat.

The kind woman who had shared her robe earlier smiled, showing her elongated teeth. Her face no longer looked as friendly as it had before. "You dare question your betters, child?"

"What're you--?"

And that's when realization dawned on Clare Lune, but it came too late. "Vampire," she whispered.

The once kindly woman swung with all her might, catching Clare off guard with a backhand that sent her flying across the courtyard to crash into the concrete barrier wall that marked the edge of the well at the center of the village. She hit with so much force that the concrete cracked under the impact.

Moon Girl was dazed, but otherwise undamaged, save for a small trickle of blood that dripped from her lip. She lifted herself up cautiously. It took a lot for her to bleed. That meant these villagers were just as dangerous as the were-creatures, if not more so. She had to tread carefully.

"Vampires," she said, spitting the word as if it were made of acid.

"That is correct, Spirit of the Moon," the vampire woman said.

"Looks like I managed to get caught in the middle of your clan war," Moon Girl said. "You know, I generally don't like taking sides in this kind of conflicts, and I know there is no love lost between *Lupas Cannes* and *the undead* but this…" and she motioned toward the carnage that surrounded them. "This is nuts even for you guys."

"I'm sorry you feel that way."

"Me too," Moon Girl said. She stood in front of the well, her hands resting behind her back.

"We are in your debt."

"You sure do have a funny way of showing it."

She released the light muzzle from his face.

The leader barked a laugh.

The vampire villagers, led by the most-honored leader, advanced toward Moon Girl. What they could not see, what they could not know, was that their Spirit of the Moon was ready for them. That familiar tingle returned and she felt the first blush of the pulsating orb of energy beginning to grown in her hands.

"You have done us a great service, child of the moon," the leader said. "So, we will honor our bargain and return you whence you came."

"You're too kind," Moon Girl quipped.

The vampire leader ignored her. "But be warned," he said with grave menace. "We are not to be trifled with. Do not pass our way again."

"Hey, I'm not the one that brought me here," Moon Girl shouted in defiance, trying to buy herself a few more seconds before she could act.

The most-honored leader, a vampire lord far older than any others of his clan, pointed his gnarled hand at Moon Girl and lightning leapt from his fingers. "You are released!" he shouted and Moon Girl began to fade away.

Nausea stabbed at her again. Teleportation again. She was, if the vampire could be believed, being returned to her apartment where they had snatched her. Of course, having had a run in or two with creatures of his ilk a time or two in the past, she knew better than to trust him completely, no matter what he said.

"Before I go," she said around a coy smile. "I've got a little something for you."

"And what might that be, child?"

"Did you know that the moon glows by reflecting the Sun's rays? Maybe not. I imagine you guys aren't too fond of the Sun. Anyway, I can do the same thing with my powers."

That got the Most Honored's attention.

"I call it a sun burst," Moon Girl said.

"No," the leader whispered as his eyes grew wide and she could see fear in them. He was beginning to understand.

"The vampires call it an explosive death."

The leader stared at her, rooted to the spot. His followers, on the other hand, turned to run, but it was too late.

"Let's just call it a going-away present," the Spirit of the Moon said with a smile.

Before the teleportation spell pulled her away, Moon Girl tossed the ball of energy she had been building behind her back into the midst of the villagers.

"Catch!"

The last thing Moon Girl saw before she was yanked away was an explosion of the brightest white light.

And then there was nothing.

Clare Lune awoke in darkness.

She was cold.

And naked.

Again.

She groaned as she sat up. She was back in her bathroom, lying on the cold tile floor. Her nose crinkled at the foul mixture of sweat, spittle, and smoke that clung to her, but at least she wasn't surrounded by creatures of the night any longer. She needed another shower, but that was a small tradeoff for being safely returned home.

As Clare sat on the edge of her bed, drying her hair, she couldn't help but wonder where she had heard the name Barrow Ridge before. Try as she might she couldn't recall where she heard the name or in what context, but she knew that she knew it.

It was damned frustrating.

Wearing only her comfy robe, Clare walked barefoot through her library and examined the wall full of bookcases filled with old tomes. The library had been passed down through her family from mother to daughter for generations, with each daughter adding to the collection. Clare herself had recently acquired some interesting volumes.

"What a night," she said to the empty apartment. As she often did when the solution to a problem eluded her, Clare worked it out loud, talking to herself. She found that verbalizing a problem helped her work out the kinks faster than quiet contemplation. "One thing still bothers me, though," she continued. "That name. Barrow Ridge. I know that name from somewhere. Why is it so familiar?"

Nearby, a particular book seemed to slide itself out from the shelf with a slight scraping sound. It caught her attention.

"What's this?"

Careful of the frail, worn pages, Moon Girl looked through the old volume. There was a passage relating to Barrow Ridge. She read the passage twice before shaking her head. She could scarcely believe her eyes.

"Unbelievable," she whispered. "I knew I recognized the name."

Just to be sure, she read the passage again. It still didn't make any sense to her, but the evidence was fairly overwhelming. When she had first read this story as a child, she had been fascinated by such mystical things like werewolves and vampires. Like most at that age, she found them fascinating. Of course, this was years before she met her first creature of the night face to face. After that encounter the romantic notions of supernatural creatures dulled and no longer held any allure for young Clare Lune.

"According to this tome," she said, reading it a fourth time. "Barrow Ridge was a center for mystical unrest in the late nineteenth century. The village was destroyed during what can only be described as an unusual solar event during a lunar eclipse."

She had been wondering *where* they had taken her with their teleportation spell.

The question she should have been asking was *when*.

"Great Luna."

Suddenly, she understood things in a way that she had not before. Over the years she had faced the vampire and werewolf clans on multiple occasions. On more than one of those instances she had been targeted by both sides as if she were some kind of war criminal. Now she was beginning to wonder if perhaps the clans did have a reason to hate her.

History told that the Lupas Cannes Clan and the Vampire Nation had both grown powerful by the late nineteenth century and were on the verge of war. It was prophesied that such a conflict would have consumed the entire planet, wiping out humanity in the process unless it was stopped.

That same history told of a natural disaster that wiped out the majority of the leaders on both sides. As a result, an uneasy truce was declared, one that existed to this day.

"My God," Clare wondered as she stepped out onto her balcony with its beautiful view of the part. She could see the Moon hanging in the clear night sky, looking to all the world as if it floated on a sea of stars.

She pulled her robe tight against a chill in the air. Nothing would ever be the same for her.

"Did I stop a war?" she wondered.

She didn't have a good answer and she was beginning to wonder if she ever would. Surely, her actions had prevented a war all those centuries ago. She had trouble wrapping her head around it. Had she really saved the world all by herself? No, she decided. The vampires had helped. It was they, after all, who had brought her there.

"Did I stop a war?" she wondered. "Or did I simply postpone the inevitable?"

It was a question that would keep her up for many nights to come.

PRIMAL INSTINCTS

THE YOUNG WARRIOR TRACKED HIS QUARRY EASILY.

For years, he had followed his father on the hunt. A great warrior and tracker in his tribe, the young warrior's father made following the beast's trail look simple. He had always believed it was easy, but now that he was on the hunt alone, he realized just how difficult the task was, and just how gifted his father was.

The tracks led to a thick copse of trees. He could hear it somewhere beyond the brush, but the echoes of the jungle made it all but impossible to pinpoint exactly where. There was a lot riding on this hunt. It was his first solo hunt. If he failed he would be sent back to apprenticeship, but even worse, his father would be humiliated that his training was lacking.

The young warrior would rather die than disappoint his father.

His grip tightening on the shaft of his spear, the young warrior stepped forward carefully. He was almost to the brush when he felt the ground tremble beneath his feet. It was a fascinating feeling, not one that he had felt before, but one that he had heard the hunters talk about before.

Stampede.

As soon as the word formed in his consciousness, the young warrior froze, his heart thundering to match the sound that seemed to come from all directions at once. He was scared and did not know which way to run.

The brush split open as if a curtain to expose the jungle beyond.

The first creature through was not the wild boar he had been tracking, but instead something much larger. The large black ape roared as it bore down on the young warrior's position.

Another followed.

Then another.

Every instinct told the boy to run away as fast as his legs would carry him, but terror held him firmly in place as the beasts headed straight toward him. If he did not move quickly they would trample him.

Suddenly, he was yanked off his feet as powerful arms wrapped around his stomach and lifted him from the ground and pulled him away from the danger. Although the boy could not see the face of his rescuer, he knew instinctively whom it was who had saved his life. "Father!" he shouted once he found his voice. The ritual was for the boy to go on the hunt alone. It was a part of the passage into becoming a man. Of course, he wasn't surprised that his father had followed him at a discreet distance. As the head of the house, his father's job was not only to feed and clothe his family, but also to keep them safe.

They ran away from the stampede, heading at an angle out of their trajectory. They stopped only when the great hunter felt it was safe to set his son back on solid ground.

They did not run far enough.

With a noise like a scream, a wild boar crashed through the brush nearby and headed straight for them. Like the apes that were likewise fleeing some unseen enemy, it was not alone. And that's when the great hunter realized that this was not a natural migration. These beasts were running away from something, some unseen enemy deep in the jungle.

The animals were afraid and their fear was going to cost the hunter and his son their lives unless they were able to get away. Thinking only of his son's life, the great hunter pushed the boy away, but it was too late. There was no place left to run.

With no time to escape, the mighty hunter and his son were trampled to death by the stampede. By the time the horde of creatures, both large and small, had passed the spot where they died, there was only a dark wet stain to mark their passing.

What neither man knew, what they couldn't know, was that this was only the beginning. Deep within the recesses of the jungle something inhuman had awakened. It growled a warning that the beasts were the first to hear and their natural instincts kicked in. They ran.

They would keep on running until there was no place left to run.

And then they would die.

"Is it always this quiet?"

Hanna Matthews stood on the prow of the antique boat called The Stacked Deck. The boat, if you could call it that, had a hand-painted image of a skeleton's hand holding five cards in its hands, a straight from the look of it, although the paint had long since started to crack and fade. The Stacked Deck was an old rust bucket with more leaks than a colander, and a smokestack that belched ugly black and gray ash into the otherwise clear sky. The captain and his two deck hands looked like something out of an old movie about smugglers or pirates so Hanna felt they truly belonged on this floating deathtrap as it chugged along the great curves of the mighty river.

Hanna gave Captain Sanchez a wide berth. Something about the man unnerved her, but then again, there wasn't much about this trip that hadn't been unsettling for a city girl like her. She had nicknamed the deck hands Hekyl and Jekyl since she didn't know their real names, not that she expected to learn them since neither of them talked very much. She had caught them sneaking glances her way when they thought she wasn't looking. They seemed fascinated by her bare legs, which were far less tanned than anyone else she had met since stepping off the plane at the small airstrip that passed for an airport. The leering didn't bother her, although she wasn't used to getting so much as a first look, much less a second one back home in the States. At first, she was flattered, but after a few hours on the boat she was starting to get creeped out by it. If there was one constant in the world, she assumed it was that men were dogs.

The sun-bleached blonde woman standing next to her said something, but Hanna had been so lost in her thoughts that she had missed it completely. "I'm sorry. What did you say?"

"I said, in answer to your question, that no, it isn't usually this quiet."

"Oh." Hanna felt her cheeks blush. She tried to hide it, but it was no use. The woman who was serving as their guide was something of a legend back where she came from. Hanna had read about her adventures and her discoveries while taking Dr. Halmstead's class back at the university. Scuttlebutt had it that she had come to the river for a research project, but that something had happened that kept her there. There were a number of theories floating around academic circles as to the reason she had gone off the reservation, but the consensus was that Petra Alexander had *"gone native."*

Hanna wasn't so certain that those rumors were quite true. She was dressed fairly normally. O Her English remained pitch perfect and she was rumored to speak at least six other languages fluently.

She was not what Hanna had been expecting. She wore jeans and a T-shirt underneath a flannel button-up shirt that she wore unbuttoned like a jacket. Hiking boots completed the ensemble. The only thing that looked native was the knife she had holstered on her belt and a second blade tucked into the side of her boot. She had long blonde hair that she kept tied up in a ponytail that made her look younger than her actual age of 30. She stood at an easy six feet, towering over Hanna's five foot five-inch frame, and although there wasn't a gym to be found within a few hundred miles, she was in fantastic shape. Her bare legs were tanned to the point of being a light brown. It made Hanna realize how much she missed her morning latte. The swill the captain served didn't deserve to be called coffee. That was when she realized that the stories she had heard were completely false. This marvelous woman hadn't gone native. No, she had simply embraced the people and their culture. It was clear from the way the locals treated her that they had embraced her as well.

Dr. Alexander was in her early thirties according to her official bio.

"Have you traveled to this area often, Dr. Alexander?" Hanna asked.

"A few times," Dr. Alexander said. "My work has been keeping me busy to the south so I haven't made the trip in quite some time." She tapped a slender finger against her chin as if searching her memory. "I'd say it's been at least two, maybe two and a half, years since I came this far north," she finally said.

"You must like it here. On the river, I mean."

"I do," she said with a smile. "I've come to think of this place as my home. Even after all this time I've only explored such a small area. I don't think you can see it all in one lifetime."

"I can't imagine living here, Dr. Alexander," Hanna said. "It's a nice place to visit, but give me concrete and coffee shops any day."

Dr. Alexander laughed. "I was that way once myself," she said. "And please, call me Petra. '*Doctor*' sounds so formal."

"Petra it is," Hanna said. "So long as you call me Hanna."

"Deal."

Hanna turned her attention back to the water ahead. "What do you think is happening out there?" she asked after a moment of silence.

Something had been causing the local wildlife to go crazy the past few weeks, but it had increased in frequency that past week. The professor's research led him to believe that the epicenter of whatever madness had infected the animals was north along the river. After checking his facts, Petra agreed.

"I wish I knew," Petra said. "I've heard of mass exoduses of animals before, but it's usually only one species or another. Having multiple herds leave at the same time is almost unheard of, especially in the timeframe Dr. Halmstead's reports indicate."

"What do you think is behind it?"

"I'm not sure," Petra said. "I saw something similar to this once. It was caused by a migration of fire ants across the plains."

"Really?" Hanna's eyes lit up.

"Of course, that was on an episode of MacGyver so I don't think it's an issue we'll have to contend with this trip." She smiled and Hanna relaxed a bit. "And if you ask me what MacGyver is it'll make me feel old so please don't."

"No worries, ma'am," Hanna said playfully. "I know what it is. My Mom owns the DVDs."

Petra groaned and then they both laughed.

"Did I miss something?" a familiar voice asked as Dr. Michael Halmstead joined them. Following behind him, as always, was Peter Anderson, the professor's aide and constant shadow.

"Just getting to know your student," Petra said.

"Ah, yes," Halmstead said. "Part of the reason I brought her along on this little jaunt. She reminds me a lot of a former gifted student of mine."

This time it was Petra's turn to blush. She nodded at the compliment.

"Captain Sanchez thinks we will reach our first stop before nightfall," Halmstead said. "He suggests we make camp there for the night then resume travel at first light."

"A wise precaution," Petra said. "The river is not the safest of places at night.Making camp on land is a good idea."

Halmstead turned to his aide. "Peter, let the captain know that he can stop for the night at our first set of coordinates."

"Yes, sir," Anderson said and headed back toward the pilot's shed.

"I have to tell you, Petra," Halmstead said. "I am excited for this trip. I was starting to think I was never going to get back out in the field again. At my age, they worry about me crossing the parking lot. Especially once I got these." He pointed to the hearing aids tucked inside each ear. "Convincing them to let me head back into the wild took some doing." He turned to face his former student. "Thank you for agreeing to join me," he said. "Had you said 'no' I have no doubt that I wouldn't be here to have this pleasant conversation."

"You know I could never say no to you, professor," Petra said. "You know that."

"Never the less, I felt it should be said."

Petra smiled. "Well, in that case, I'm glad you're here. It's been too long since we had a chance to chat and catch up."

Hanna sat back and listened to their stories. Professor Halmstead had spoken often of Petra Alexander. Some of the stories seemed far-fetched on the surface, but now that she had the opportunity to meet the woman in person, she wasn't so sure that dismissing her adventures out of hand was the right play. If nothing else, her presence had certainly had a profound effect on the professor. He seemed more energetic than he had in months. He had the glow of a man in love. Whether that love came from being around the beautiful Dr. Alexander or just the thrill of being back in the field again, she couldn't say. Whatever the reason, she had never seen the man so happy.

"Whatever's out there, we'll find it," Halmstead said enthusiastically.

"I hope you're right," Petra said, her voice soft. "Too many people have died already."

Morning came quickly.

As with every morning since they arrived, the expedition team rose early, ate a sparse breakfast, then freshened up a bit before breaking camp and getting back on their way. Captain Sanchez and his men already had the boat engines revved up and ready to go, as evidenced by the black smoke that chugged skyward.

Dr. Alexander stretched her tired muscles before stowing her gear. As much as she enjoyed sleeping on the ground, she noticed that there were a few aches and pains that came with doing so that hadn't been there when she first arrived on this beautiful continent. There were many things a person could hide from in the wilds of the jungle, but getting older was unfortunately not one of them.

By the time the sun had just started to peek over the tops of the trees they had already gone a mile up river. The captain's boat didn't look like much, but aesthetics aside, it was a sturdy vessel with powerful engines and they were making good time.

"Stop the boat!" She recognized it as Professor Halmstead's voice from somewhere near the front of the boat. An experienced explorer, Petra knew that the man was not prone to shouting unless it was serious. She ran forward, pushing her way past the professor's aide, who had zero skills when it came to being on a boat. Not for the first time, she wondered why Halmstead had brought Peter Anderson along.

"What is it?" Petra shouted as she came upon the professor and Hanna Matthews. They were looking over the railing at something in the water.

"There's someone out there," Hanna shouted.

Petra leaned over and saw that she was right. A body was floating facedown in the muddy water. A man's body, he had become tangled in some roots that held him in place. Petra grabbed a pole with a hook on it and marched forward just in time to see Hanna kick off her shoes and remove her outer shirt.

"What are you doing?" Petra asked.

"I'm going to get him."

"I wouldn't do that," she said.

"Why not?" Hanna's expression was one of confusion. "I'm an excellent swimmer."

"Doesn't matter," Petra explained. "The currents don't look bad, but there are severe undertows that have been known to suck a person down without warning."

"Seriously?"

"Yes," Halmstead said. "She's right. It's much too dangerous."

"Plus, you never know what nasty critter might be waiting for you down there," Petra added as she used the hook to catch onto the dead man's clothing and pull him up. Captain Sanchez helped her haul the body onto the deck. Along with the large snake that had taken refuge inside the dead man's clothing.

Using the hook and pole, she flipped the snake back into the water where it quickly disappeared beneath the brown water.

Hanna looked like she wanted to throw up at the sight of the reptile. "Thank you," she managed to say.

"Don't worry about it," Petra said before kneeling down next to the dead man. His body was a crumpled mess. "Looks like he's been dead at least a couple of days," she said in answer to the unspoken question.

"What happened to him?" Peter Anderson asked.

Petra pointed at the various bruises and broken bones. "From the look of the broken bones and bruise pattern, I'd guess he was trampled."

"A stampede?" Hanna asked.

"Of a fashion, Miss Matthews," Halmstead said, slipping easily into teaching mode. "It's not unusual for large herds of animals to mass migrate to other parts of the continent. It is all simply part of their life cycle, wouldn't you agree, Dr. Alexander?"

"I would. Although, the locals usually have time to get out of their path," she said. "This guy looks like he was caught right in the middle of it."

"It looks like he was not alone," Peter said.

"What was that, Mr. Anderson?" Halmstead asked.

Peter Anderson pointed toward the water ahead. "Looks like this guy had plenty of company."

They stood and joined him at the front of the boat. All along the quarter mile stretch between them and the next fork in the river floated dozens of bodies, each surrounded by a small pool of red that stood out in stark contrast to the brown of the muddy river.

"What could have done this?" the professor asked.

"Could it be smugglers?" Anderson asked. "Or pirates? You hear all kinds of stories about bandits being active on the river."

"I don't think so," Petra said.

"How can you be sure?" the young man asked.

"In my experience, smugglers usually shoot their victims. It's just simple," Petra said as she knelt once again next to the body. "This guy doesn't have a single bullet hole in him."

"Oh. Sorry," Anderson said, his cheeks blushing with embarrassment.

"Don't be," she said. "Science is all about asking questions. Never apologize for that."

"I-- I won't," he said.

"Good. So, if not smugglers, then we're looking at a probable animal attack," Petra said. "Several rather large animals in fact."

"So, that brings us back to stampede," Halstead added. "With whatever strange has been happening out here, there's too many dead people and animals have been found down river for this to be a coincidence.

"That would be my guess," Petra said. "What I don't understand is why they didn't run?"

"Maybe they didn't have time," Hanna said as she slipped back on her shoes.

"Maybe," Petra said, cupping her chin as she processed the information. "I mean, it is possible, but…"

"But what?"

"A herd on the move travels fairly slowly so as not to leave any of the slower members behind. They also make a great deal of noise," Petra explained. "It's hard not to hear them coming. That begs an important question."

"Which is?"

"The herd could have been running," Petra guessed.

"Such a thing is not unheard of," Halmstead chimed in.

"He is right," Sanchez added. "I have seen it with my own eyes. Very nasty business."

"So, what made them run?"

"That's a very good question, Hanna," Petra said. "A very good question indeed. The answer lies upstream."

"What about the bodies?" Hanna asked.

"There's nothing we can do for them now," Halmstead answered. "The best we can do is call in their location and see if another boat can be dispatched to pick up the remains." He turned to Sanchez. "May I borrow your radio, Captain?"

"Of course, Professor. This way."

Hanna stood next to Petra and stared at the bodies floating peacefully on the water. "Do you think they'll send a boat out here to pick them up?" she asked after a moment of silence.

"I don't know," Petra said. "Maybe." Her voice trailed off for a moment before she added, "I doubt it."

"I hate this place," Hanna whispered.

Petra didn't comment.

The next few hours were uneventful.

When they heard the roar of some distant beast, everyone snapped to and ran up on deck to see if they could catch a glimpse of whatever had captured their attention.

"There!" Hanna shouted and pointed.

The others were immediately at her side, looking in the direction indicated. The trees swayed violently back and forth, despite the fact that there was no wind. The river was as calm as they had seen it. Whatever was happening Enland was not a weather anomaly.

"Can you make out any details?" Halmstead asked as Captain Sanchez maneuvered the boat closer to shore.

"No," Petra said. "It sounds like--"

Before she could finish a man burst free of the jungle into a small clearing not far from the water's edge. Large trees hung out over the river, which kept the boat from coming all the way to shore. Vines hung from the tallest branches. Whoever the man was, he was terrified.

"Help me!" he shouted as soon as he saw the boat. "They're coming!"

Sanchez's men were on the move without so much as a word from their captain. The Stacked Deck was stocked with several small inflatable rafts that came in handy at times like this one when the larger boat could not reach land. The only problem was that it took time to get them out of storage below decks, carry them back up on deck, then inflate and get them in the water.

That was time the man on shore did not have.

Petra removed her flannel shirt, revealing a bikini top, and dropped it to the deck next to several rolls of rope that were stowed on board in case they were needed. Petra scooped up a small spool of rope and ran toward the back of the boat. She was halfway up the ladder to the upper turret that housed the captain shed before anyone realized what she was doing.

"Where's…" Hanna asked, but the words dried out in her throat before she could complete the thought.

Petra unrolled the rope and tied a quick not that created a lasso that she then threw into the trees that kept The Stacked Deck from getting closer to shore. She snagged a tall branch on her second attempt. A few quick tugs told her that it would support her weight.

"Is she insane?" Peter asked from below as he watched her test the rope.

"What is she doing?" Hanna asked.

Before anyone could answer, Petra leapt from the captain's shed as if taking a swan dive into the river. Hanna wanted to scream for her to stop as the memory of the snake inside the dead man's clothes earlier filled her mind.

Still holding the rope, Petra soared until the slack pulled tight and her fall became an arc that carried her just inches above the water before snatching her back into the air and carried her toward shore. Working out the math in her head, she released her grip and dropped to the dry earth, landing in a crouch that turned into a roll that slowed her momentum.

"Are you okay?" she asked the stranger.

He looked at her as if he had never laid eyes on a woman before.

"Hello," she said. "Earth to…"

That's when the creatures they couldn't see bellowed their anger once more and the ground beneath them began to shake violently. The vibrations were so strong that neither of them could keep their footing and they both fell to the ground.

Leaves rustled and trees collapsed under the weight of the troop of black-furred gorillas that tore through the jungle into the clearing. There were six of them bearing down on Petra and the man she had tried to save. Whatever had spooked them, the gorillas were in a state of blind panic. They were terrified and that terror caused them to lash out at whatever they felt might be cause.

The presence of two humans was all the provocation they needed.

Petra was on the move, pushing the man forward just ahead of the massive fists that slammed the ground where they had been only an instant before. "Go! Run!" she shouted.

"Where?"

"There!" Petra pointed to the water where she could see the deck hands just getting the life raft into the water. "Head for the raft!"

"What about you?"

Petra looked up at the limbs above her as her mind raced through multiple calculations. "I'll keep them busy until you're clear," she said.

"But…"

"No buts! Just go!" she said with authority.

The alpha male of the group, sneered at her, saliva dripping from his mouth. By the time he let loose with a war cry Petra was already on the move. She ran in the opposite direction of the river's edge, instead heading back into the bush. The gorillas followed.

Petra scurried up a tree as though she were part squirrel and ran across the limbs as though she were not a couple dozen feet off the ground. The alpha male roared in fury, shaking his fists in the air. Petra rested a moment on a high branch, surprised that they hadn't followed her up the tree yet. Or worse, simply pushed it over. With their combined strength, it would be child's play.

The fact that they seemed more afraid than angry was enough to convince Petra that they were on the right track. Whatever was causing the animals to stampede was obviously upstream. Now all she had to do was get back on the boat and out of the alpha male gorilla's line of sight.

When the alpha finally pushed aside his fear, he charged the tree.

Petra held tight as a tremor quaked through the old wood that sent leaves flowing all about the ground below. When she saw the beast raise its arms for another blow, she made her move. Petra leapt from the branch and grabbed hold of one in the next tree over.

She lost her balance, but quickly recovered.

She let out a breath and searched through the leaves for any sign of the rope she had used to get from the boat. Below, she saw that the man she had rescued was now in the raft and halfway back to the boat.

The rope was hard to see among the dense leaves and various branches, but she found it. Unfortunately, she couldn't reach it from where she was at the moment. There wasn't time to plan her next move because the tree began to sway and bend. She looked down and saw one of the gorillas climbing up to get her.

"Time to go," Petra said before taking a deep breath and leaping across the space between the trees.

Her hands snagged the rope and slid down a foot before stopping. Her skin burned, but she held tight and kicked off from the tree and swung out over the water toward the boat. Much like she had done before, she released her grip and tumbled onto the deck of The Stacked Deck. This time her landing was somewhat less graceful than before and she landed on her butt.

"Are you okay?" she heard Hanna Matthews shout.

"I'll live," Petra responded through the pain in her hands. Strips of flesh had torn free from the rope burn. "It's okay, Hanna," she said after seeing the look on the girl's face. "It looks worse than it really is. Trust me."

Professor Halmstead knelt next to her, a first aid kit clutched in his hand. He pulled an antiseptic spray from the box and sprayed it on the wounds, which nearly brought tears to Petra's eyes. She bit her lip until he had finished cleaning the wound and wrapped her hands. By that time the medicated spray had done its work and she felt no pain in her hands.

"How's our guest?" she asked the professor.

"Grateful," the man said from nearby. He stuck out a hand, then pulled it back when he remembered her bandaged hands. "My name is Lionel Martindale. I can't thank you enough for saving my life back there."

"A pleasure to meet you, sir," Petra said with a nod. "I am curious what you were doing so far out in the jungle all by yourself."

"I wasn't by myself," Martindale explained. His voice trailed off as he added, "At least not at first."

"What happened?" Halmstead asked.

"I work for the Ellis Enland Hydroelectric Plant," he explained. "It's about twenty miles upriver."

"I've heard of that," Hanna said. The others turned to look at her, which made her blush slightly. "Uh… I read some articles about it when I was researching the trip," she added.

"It's big news in these parts as well," Captain Sanchez said. "Many in my country protested this giant man-made monstrosity being built."

"What happened?" Hanna asked.

"The same thing that always happens, little one," Sanchez said. "Money changes hands and the objections of the people are ignored in favor of exotic guest homes on a white sandy beach somewhere."

"That's a pretty cynical view of how things work," Peter said.

"Maybe so, Mr. Anderson, but an accurate one in this part of the world," Petra said. "However, it's not politics or greed that has brought us here today. What happened out there, Mr. Martindale? Do you know what has spooked the animals?"

"I have no idea."

"Then why were you out here?"

Martindale sighed. "Look, I'm just an engineer on the project. The first substation went on-line three days ago. Everything seemed to be running smoothly at first."

"But…" Petra prodded.

"Something odd happened during the first eighteen hours of operation," Martindale said. "We had a drop in power from the substation. We knew that fluctuations were to be expected, but this was a significant drop. Before the main plant could go on-line, we had to make sure the substations were operating at maximum efficiency."

"So, what you're saying is that the substations are what is used to power the main plant?" Halmstead asked.

"Yes. One substation is not enough to power the main plant. At best it only creates twenty to twenty-five percent power. It's enough to start the turbines, but not enough to run them efficiently. Part of our deal with the government was to build a plant that did not radically deplete local resources."

Captain Sanchez snorted his derision.

"Keep going," Petra prompted.

"Right," Martindale said. "When the power output dropped to nine percent the start up for the main plant was put on hold until we could determine what had happened to cause the power drop. Substation two was started up to make up for the power fluctuations coming from station one. I was sent out with a team to inspect the substation and make a report back to my superiors."

"What did you find?" Halstead asked.

"What did I find?" Martindale said with a laugh. "You saw what I found." He pointed toward shore. "Those giant monkeys were doing their best King Kong impression on the substation. They inflicted some heavy damage. We managed to get inside, but they came after us. My team… my team was killed and I… well, I ran. I've been running since then. I thought I was a goner for sure."

"How far are we away from this substation of yours?"

"Not far. Maybe a couple of miles."

Petra turned to Halmstead. "With your permission, I think we need to make a detour."

"Of course," the professor said.

"Good," Petra said. "Captain, we need to make a course change."

The substation had seen better days.

At Dr. Alexander's insistence, she had gone ashore alone with Martindale. Her thinking was that if any of their big furry friends were still in the area and they had to make a run for the boat, it would be a lot easier if there were only two of them. Reluctantly, Professor Halmstead agreed, although it was clear that he was itching to get a look at the damage himself.

Conversely, Martindale looked like he would rather have been anyplace else. If not for the fact that she needed his expertise, Petra would have gladly left him on the boat where it was safe.

"Those gorillas did all this?" she asked.

"I think so," he said. "A lot of the damage had already been done by the time we got here. If I hadn't seen it with my own eyes I would have assumed it was the locals trying to prevent the main station from going on-line."

"There have been threats?"

"Oh, yes," he said. "A lot of them. The company increased security at the main plant, but they didn't think anything about these unmanned substations, as you can see."

"Is there anything in here that might agitate the animals?" Petra asked as they made their way through the damaged substation.

"Beats me," Martindale said. "Nothing I can think of, but I'm an engineer, not a veterinarian."

"What about the noise?"

"I'm not sure I follow?"

"I'm sure this thing makes a good bit of noise," Petra said, tapping a knuckle against the metal and listening to the sound echo all around them.

"Not as much as you might think. It's fairly quiet. Just a slight hum," he offered. "Why do you ask?"

"Animal hearing is a bit more sensitive than ours," Petra explained. "I was just working up a possible hypothesis."

At roughly the size of a small hut many of the nearby villagers lived in, the substation was small and compact. The prefabricated metal building housed various pumps, valves, and a computerized monitoring system. Martindale explained that the pumps were designed to pull water from various sections of the river and run them along the pipeline that connected the substation to the main plant. By pulling water from various sections of the river, the company believed that the natural resources the local politicians were interested in preserving would be impacted less than if pulled from one single section of the river. The runoff from the turbines would be pumped back into the river upstream. The engineer explained that the water they returned to the river would be cleaner than that which they removed.

Petra wasn't quite sure she believed that or not.

Martindale pinched the bridge of his nose between his thumb and forefinger. A soft groan escaped his lips.

"You okay?"

"Yeah," he said. "I'm fine. Just a little headache, that's all."

"Let's get back to the boat, okay?" she said. Petra glanced around at the surroundings. There was jungle on all sides of the substation, even though much of it had been trampled. From the tracks she was able to make out it was clear that the gorillas they had encountered were not the only critters to pass through the area in recent days. Offhand she counted at least six distinct print types.

Something else worried her. She hadn't heard a single bird for hours. Even the natural chirps and clicks of the native insects had gone quiet. She hadn't even spotted the first ant since she set foot on dry land. That in and of itself was enough to give her pause. If there was one constant on the river, it was that the ants ruled the land. They were everywhere.

"I like that idea," Martindale said, relieved to hear that they were heading back to the boat. "This place gives me the willies."

"I know what you mean," she said. She didn't want to alarm the engineer, but something had set her skin tingling. It was a feeling she couldn't shake. It was as if she were being watched by a predator that she couldn't see, but she did feel its eyes on her. She had to fight back the urge to run, which made her wonder if the indigenous population had felt it as well.

It was a terrifying thought. Petra had seen many things in the jungle, many of them quite difficult to explain, some that almost appeared supernatural. Petra was not a believer, but she was keenly aware that the river held many secrets and most of them were deadly. However, the headache forming behind her eyes did make her wonder.

The Ellis Enland Hydroelectric Plant loomed large before them.

The plant was massive, a testament to human ingenuity and will power. Many had tried to tame the jungle over the centuries, but they had all failed. Only those who chose to live in harmony with the ecosystem seemed to thrive in this environment. Many believed that the jungle was alive. Petra Alexander agreed with that notion, although she drew the line at calling it a singular entity. The river consisted of millions of independent life forms working toward a common goal, protecting the rainforest and its mighty river.

The Ellis Enland Corporation had thus far succeeded where so many before had failed. They had pushed back the jungle and supplanted it with an edifice of concrete and steel that had the potential to change the course of the mighty River.

The thought terrified the locals.

Petra understood this. As a scientist, she understood the need to grow and advance the cause of human civilization, but since she first came to this place, she had come to understand just how sacred this place was to those who called it home. She had added herself to the roster of those who swore to protect it.

Captain Sanchez docked the boat and his deck hands quickly tied it off. Just as they stepped off onto the dock, a group of three men raced toward them. The one in the three-piece suit was obviously in charge, most likely a representative sent by the home office. The second man wore khakis and shirtsleeves rolled up to the elbows. The third man was uniformed security.

"I'm Rupert Marsh," the man in the suit said. He offered his hand, first to Martindale, then to Halmstead, and finally Petra. The others had remained on board.

Hanna and Peter were grabbing their gear, refusing to stay on the boat. "We came here for some hands on research," Hanna reminded her professor.

"It doesn't get much more hands on than this." He had agreed that they could join the group.

"Are you okay, Lionel?" the man in shirtsleeves asked. "We were worried."

"I'm fine, Mike," Martindale said. "Thanks to these folks."

"Forgive my manners," Mike said. "Name's Mike Loggins. I'm the foreman here. Thanks for bringing our man back to us."

Neither man introduced the security guard, but Petra noticed that his nametag had *Marsters* engraved on it. She introduced the group, starting with Halmstead and ending with Peter.

"What brings you out to our neck of the woods?" Marsh asked as he escorted them toward the plant's office. His words were friendly, but the tone was just accusatory enough that she noticed.

"We're investigating mysterious behavior by some of the local wildlife," Halmstead. "I'm afraid there have been some deaths."

"I was almost one of them," Martindale added.

"We've not had any wildlife troubles here," Loggins said. "In fact, it's been rather quiet the past few days."

"Since substation one went active, perhaps?" Petra queried.

Loggins thought about it. "Maybe. To be honest, I've been so busy getting this place ready for launch that I've not really paid all that much attention."

"What are you insinuating, Doctor Alexander?"

"Well, Mr. Marsh, based on the evidence we've collected and the incident locations, we believe that your plant is ground zero for whatever is running off the animals."

"That's preposterous," Marsh said.

"Are you certain, absolutely and without question sure that you're not unknowingly responsible?" Hanna asked.

"Of course I am," Marsh barked. "Young lady, this is a multi-million dollar project. I assure you, every possible precaution has been taken."

Petra saw the foreman grimace slightly. "Do you agree with that, Mr. Loggins?"

He said nothing.

"Loggins?" Marsh asked, the blood draining from his face.

"Well?" Petra prompted.

"I don't know," Loggins said. "It could be nothing."

"But it could also be something," Halmstead added. "You need to tell us, son."

"Loggins?" Marsh asked again. "What's going on?"

"I don't know for sure, Mr. Marsh, but there has been something weird going on since we initiated the reactor's start up routine."

"What?"

"I reported it, sir," Loggins added. "I was told that it was within tolerances."

"What is it?" Petra asked.

"Perhaps you'd better come with me," Loggins said and hurried off.

"Good idea," Petra said, then followed.

"You wouldn't happen to have any aspirin, would you?" she heard Peter ask the security guard. "I've got a killer headache."

They stood on a platform overlooking the dam.

"The building that houses the plant was originally a cannery that had been built forty years earlier by a Brazillian businessman who thought he could bring jobs and income to the area," Loggins said. "His business failed and the building sat empty for decades until Ellis Enland bought it. The building was reinforced and we've added new buildings as upgrades have been implemented. Our size has increased by a factor of ten."

"What does any of this have to do with our problem?" Halmstead asked.

"The original dam was built using the original building as part of its foundation," Loggins continued. "There have been concerns from both the engineering department and the builder that it might not be up to the task, especially once we fill it to capacity, which has never been done before."

"And you reported this?"

"Repeatedly," Loggins said, casting a glance toward Rupert March. "Our concerns were met with less than enthusiastic responses."

"This place has passed all of the inspections and met all of the required safety measures as required by the government. They are content with our safety, Mr. Loggins. Why aren't you?"

"Maybe you haven't been paying attention, but people are dying out there," Petra said.

"That has nothing to do with us," Marsh protested. "Aside from the problems with Substation One, everything is running as planned. We have two additional substations running without a hitch."

Martindale couldn't believe what he was hearing. "Wait. You started station three before I finished my investigation? I almost died out there and you couldn't be bothered to wait until I got back?"

"Yes, we did," Marsh said. "This project is on a timetable and I aim to meet it. Deadlines wait for no man. Not even you, Mr. Martindale."

"You sonuva--"

Before the angry engineer could say another word, Professor Halmstead let out a pained scream and dropped to his knees, his face resting in his hands. Blood dripped from his hands and from his ears.

"Professor?" Petra was at his side. "His nose is bleeding. Someone hand me a towel or a shirt." Hanna handed over a small cloth and Petra pressed it against the nose to pinch off the flow. "Hold still," she said.

"My ears," the professor whispered. "It's so... so loud."

Hanna was the first to understand. "His hearing aids. He has them turned up pretty loud. It's the only way he can hear!"

"What's he hearing that we aren't?" Marsh demanded as Petra removed the devices from his ears. The professor blew out a breath the moment they were removed and slumped to the ground.

Petra held the tiny device next to her own ear and could make out the faint whistle. "Ow!" she said. "It's some kind of whine. Very high pitched. That's probably why we can't hear it, at least not on a conscious level. It's probably why we've all got headaches."

"I bet the animals hear it," Hanna added.

Petra snapped her fingers. "Right. The wildlife hears a higher range than we do. That could be what's driving them mad."

"What's causing it?" Loggins asked.

"Is it a natural occurrence?" Marsh asked.

"Doubtful," Petra replied. "Mr. Loggins, can your monitoring equipment measure sound waves?"

"With a few modifications, I think so."

"Let's find out. I have a very bad feeling," Petra said.

"Do you know what's going on?" Hanna asked.

"I think so, but God, I hope I'm wrong."

"What is it?" Marsh asked.

"You've got a crack," Petra said as if that explained everything.

"Don't be absurd!"

"I hope I'm wrong, but what if I'm not?" Petra argued. "If you fill this dam without making sure and the dam bursts, you could flood the entire river. There are thousands of people who live and work along this river. A flood would wipe them all out."

"You're asking me to halt a multi-million dollar deal on nothing but conjecture, Doctor!"

"But it's conjecture that fits the facts," Petra said.

"What if she's right, Rupert?" Loggins asked. "Can we really take that chance?"

"Hanna, get everyone to the boat," Petra ordered. "We're going to shut this thing down."

"You are not," Marsh said decisively.

"Try and stop me," Petra dared him before running with Loggins and Martindale toward the control center.

They were almost there when the first quake hit.

The ground bucked beneath them, throwing each of them to the concrete.

"That's not good," Petra muttered as she got back to her feet. "We have to hurry," she told the others.

"You'll get no argument from me," Loggins said. "You really think there's a crack in the dam causing this?"

"It's just a guess, but based on the way this place is shaking, I'd say it's a good one. Something similar happened with a dam in Maine a couple years back. Thankfully, it was caught in time."

A loud splintering sound caught their attention and as one they turned to watch as a crack worked its way through the concrete floor and up one of the walls of the control building.

"Oh, that's not good," Martindale said.

"No, it's not. We've got to move," Petra shouted and together they ran for the building's employee entrance.

As soon as they reached it, Loggins swiped his card to unlock the door.

Nothing happened.

He tried again.

Still nothing.

"Is there another way in?" Petra asked as she watched a new crack snap and pop its way across the once flat surface.

"The main entrance is on the other side of the building. All of the access doors only open from the inside," Martindale informed her.

"That'll take too long," Petra said. "We need another way in there fast."

Loggins pointed to a third story window. "How about through there?"

"That'll have to do," Petra said as she looked for something to use. She plucked the telescoping baton from the security guard's belt. "Looks like I've got a key. You keep trying to get that door open while I try plan B."

"How are you going to get up there?" Loggins asked, but she was already on the move, shimmying up a drainage pipe to the second floor.

"Trust me," Martindale said. "This lady has some moves."

Petra pushed off from the building and grabbed hold of the railing for the second-floor patio. She made it look effortless as she pulled herself up then flipped over the wall onto the deck. She looked up. Getting to the third story window would be a bit trickier. There were fewer handholds. She got a running start the leapt onto the patio wall. With a flick of the wrist she opened the guard's wand and swung it at the window with all her strength.

The glass shattered on the third strike.

Suddenly, she was glad to have the bandages wrapped around her hands. It would help her with the glass pieces still lodged in the windowsill. With no time to waste, Petra leapt toward the window and grabbed the sill with one hand, but not both. She swung away from the building, wildly off balance, but she managed to get hold with her other hand and pull herself in.

The control room was small and thankfully everything was labeled. She looked around the room for the right button until she saw it at the far end of the room. She ran to the emergency shut off valve, lifted the clear plastic protective covering, and slammed it shut with the palm of her hand.

Everything went silent.

Petra sank to the floor and blew out a breath.

Petra Alexander stood on the observation platform and watched as work crews started their descent into the dam. The whine that had been picked up by the professor's hearing aids had subsided and scanning teams were already in the process of trying to find the cause of the sound. Despite his continued stance that the power plant was not the source of the troubles, Rupert Marsh had agreed to the additional tests.

"Enjoying the view, Doctor?" Mike Loggins asked as he stepped up beside her.

"Just glad there's still something here to see, Mr. Loggins," Petra said.

"So am I."

"I wanted to thank you for standing up to your boss back there," she said. "That took courage."

"Not really," Loggins said. "What was the worst thing he could do to me, fire me? I've been unemployed before."

"It was still a big risk so thank you."

"Do you really think they'll find a crack in the dam?"

"I'm not sure," she said. "Something in this structure was causing the noise. If it's not a crack, then it's something else. Of course, since the tremors hit there are plenty of new cracks that will have to be sealed."

"Looks like we've got our work cut out for us."

"Whatever it was that started all of this, the local wildlife knew enough to head for the hills," Petra said. "If the stampede hadn't happened this could have been disastrous."

"Guess we've still got a thing or two to learn from the beasts, huh, Doctor?"

"Yeah. And please, it's Petra. Doctor sounds so... formal."

"Petra it is," Loggins said. "So long as you make sure it's Mike."

Petra smiled. "I think I can handle that... Mike."

"I guess you'll be heading back pretty soon?"

"Yes," Petra said. "I'm not built for all this concrete and steel. Not anymore. Give me dirt, bugs, and big ol' trees any day."

Mike laughed at the comment. "Maybe I'll come by and visit you."

"Won't you be busy here for the foreseeable future?"

"For a little while," Mike said. "But I know how the game is played. I went up against management. It doesn't matter if I was right or not, Ellis Enland doesn't look too favorably on folks doing that sort of thing. Once things have quieted down I fully expect Lionel and I will be quietly let go."

"That's horrible," Petra said.

"If it's any consolation, Marsh will probably get tossed out on his ass too," he said with a wink.

"Oddly enough, that does make me feel a little better," Petra said.

They laughed.

"In all seriousness," she added. "If you find yourself unemployed with a little time to kill, stop by the lab and see me. I'd love to give you the tour of my river. It'll make you forget all about this place."

"Now that sounds like a good plan, Doc."

This time Petra gave him a wink.

Petra Alexander gave Professor Halmstead a big hug.

"It was great to see you again, sir," she said.

"Always a pleasure, my dear," he said. "If you ever find yourself eager to return to the States, just give me a call and I'll make it happen."

"You'll be my first call," she told him.

The effects from the high frequency sound that had ruptured blood vessels in his nose and ears caused no lasting damage, a fact for which she was extremely grateful. She watched as her old mentor carried his own bag to the plane, his ever-present shadow, Peter Anderson in place at his side.

She smiled as she watched them go.

"I'm actually going to miss this place," Hanna Matthews said from nearby.

Petra chuckled.

"Yeah. I can't believe I said it either," Hanna joked.

"I told you this place grows on you," Petra said.

"I guess you were right."

"If you ever want to come back and do some studies in the area, I have a friend that would be happy to offer you a grant. Just say the word and I'll make it happen," Petra said, smiling when she realized that she sounded very much like her former professor.

"Really?" Hanna beamed. "I might just take you up on that." She hugged Petra.

"Be good, Hanna," Petra said as the student ran to catch up with the others.

"So, you have a friend with grant money, eh?" Captain Sanchez said as he moved up next to Petra.

"Well, I like to think I'm a friendly person, Captain."

"Of course, Doctor Alexander. Of course."

"Watch it, buster or there'll be no tip for you," Petra said playfully as they headed back toward the boat which would return her to the lab she called home.

Sanchez laughed and she couldn't help but join him.

SHOWDOWN AT BROKEN EAGLE

TOMMY GLUTCH AWOKE SURROUNDED BY DARKNESS.

His eyes, normally so quick to adjust to darkness, failed to respond. The smell of moisture and mildew mixed with a burnt smell that was not wood or coal. Wherever he was, it was underground. He tried to move, but something lay atop him, something heavy. *I've been buried alive*, his brain screamed. He pushed against the weight, felt it move, then redoubled his efforts.

That's when the object that had been lying across him moaned.

He recognized the voice immediately.

"Darryl?"

"Izzat you, baby brother?" Darryl Glutch said, his voice cracking hard.

"It's me. Get offa me, why don't ya?"

Slowly, the brothers got to their feet, careful to make sure they didn't bump their heads on anything. An eerie red light filled the space everywhere Tommy looked. "Where are we?" he asked, not expecting an answer.

"Hell," came a weak reply from nearby. "We're in hell."

"Pa!" Darryl and Tommy lurched across the room until they saw him. Their father lay on the ground, his body broken and battered. Shards of broken bone reflected the red light that seemed to follow them.

"Mah boys," the white-haired cowboy said, a milky pink spittle rolling from the left side of his mouth that would no longer close completely. His leg had been crushed under a large rock. To see Jedediah Glutch, a man who was once the most powerful man Tommy had ever known, broken was almost more than he could bear.

"Who did this do to ya, Pa?"

"Strangers," their Pa said, his voice crackled much like Darryl's had, only worse. "Strangers came to… Broken Eagle. They did this to us." He motioned toward the darkness beyond his reach. "To all of us."

Tommy stood and walked forward, the damnable red light illuminating his path. He came to a ledge overlooking a deep pit. He looked down and what he saw threatened to freeze him to his core. The townspeople of Broken Eagle, those he had known all his life, lay at the bottom of the pit. *Massacred.*

Returning to his father's side, Tommy grabbed the man by his broken hand. "They got everyone, Pa. The whole town."

"Can't let them get… away with… it," Jedediah said, his voice catching on the words before he finally fell silent with only a soft buzz of breath to indicate his presence. The Glutch brothers said goodbye to their father then stayed by his side until the light went out of his eyes and the buzzing fell still.

"Now what?" Darryl asked.

Hands balled into fists, Tommy Glutch stood. "Now we do what Pa asked. We go home and find these strangers. Then we take back what's rightfully ours."

"How do we do that, Tommy, with just the two of us?"

Tommy looked around the crimson-tinged cavern.

"I guess we'd better dig us up some help."

PART 1: WHAT WAS...

Broken Eagle, Arizona.
Population: varies.

A BOOMING TOWN WHEN GOLD WAS FIRST STRUCK, THE TOWN OF BROKEN Eagle fell into disrepair quickly after the veins dried up and the mass exodus began. Almost overnight, the prospectors, miners, businessmen, shop owners, and dreamers all moved on in search of the next shiny rock they could polish and sell to make their fortunes.

It was a wonder that newcomers still found themselves passing beneath the wooden sign hanging from the rotted wood gate posts at the edge of town, but every so often visitors found themselves in Broken Eagle.

Three strangers, Terrance Mallory and his aides, Tim Conrad and Martin Seltz, strode into town. Unlike the rough and tumble cowpokes they saw on the streets, the three newcomers were clean. Their clothes were pristine and new and not yet caked with dust and mud like the locals. Each of them sported a gun belt with a shiny new pistol on each hip.

They pass the signpost and Mallory chuckled as he read the dwindling numbers on a small wooden sign. It read: *BROKEN EAGLE, ARIZONA POP. 1000 - 600 - 500 - 100 - 75 - 60...* Each number had been scratched out in favor of a new, lower count. If he wasn't already aware that Broken Eagle was well on its way to becoming a ghost town, one look around painted a pretty ominous picture.

The Sheriff's Office was the first building on Broken Eagle's lone street. No light flickered through the window from inside. A sign leaned against the cobweb-covered glass. It read: *Closed.* Mallory didn't know the story well, but he had heard rumors that Broken Eagle had been without permanent law for some time.

"All the places you could have visited, sir," Tim Conrad said. "And this is the place you choose?"

Mallory couldn't contain his boyish grin, which looked out of place on his deep-lined face. Years of working behind a desk had aged him more than he would have ever dreamt. Stepping away from the office for the chance to run off and "*play cowboy*" had been the smartest decision he'd ever made.

"Can you think of anyplace better?"

"Yes."

Mallory laughed. "Trust me. You're going to love this," he said even as he increased his stride, eager to start their new adventure.

"I doubt it, sir."

"Why this place?" Martin Seltz asked.

"Why not?" Mallory said.

"If you don't mind my saying so, sir, but this doesn't seem the safest of places to visit," Seltz said.

"It's not, Martin. Even in its prime, Broken Eagle wasn't a nice town by any means," Mallory explained, gesturing at the decaying buildings all around him. "When the respectable citizens left to pursue their dreams of striking it rich, only the lowest of the low remained behind. Crooks, cheats, liars, hookers, dreamers, moon shiners, card players, and the profiteers who feed off them. Those are the folks who call this place home."

"But why would--"

Before the aide could continue his question, a loud crash caught their attention from a nearby building. It was the only establishment on Main Street that looked to be open.

"The saloon," Mallory said, instantly changing course and making a beeline for the saloon entrance. "Perfect."

Before he could reach the three steps that led to the entrance, the commotion from inside reached a fevered pitch and a man was thrown backwards through the saloon's big picture window. Glass rained into the dusty dirt street as the man hit the ground hard.

Mallory was reminded that Broken Eagle was not the safest place to hang your hat.

Especially if you're the law.

Mallory saw the man and caught sight of the Federal U.S. Marshal's badge pinned to his blue pressed shirt. As he suspected, this was not some local sheriff trying to break up a bar fight. The Marshal was hunting something more dangerous. Or he had tried to arrest the wrong person. Around Broken Eagle, such things were simply not done. And never attempted alone. This town had become a safe-haven for wicked men. Any marshal crazy-- or stupid-- enough to walk into this town alone was not long for this world.

Marshal James Fallon wasn't crazy and he wasn't stupid.

What he was, however, was outgunned.

And he'd managed to cross the wrong man.

An honorable man, James Fallon believed in justice. It was a noble trait for a Federal Marshal, but it often got him in trouble. Riding into a cesspool of a town like Broken Eagle to arrest Horrigan, the local overlord, without back up was not his smartest plan.

Horrigan was a big man, all muscle. There were few faster than him on the draw and even fewer with a shorter fuse on their temper. Sometimes all it took was a cross look to send the man into a violent rage. His reputation for violence had become almost legendary even as far as two states away.

Although it wasn't Horrigan's given first name, someone had hung the nickname of "Black Bart" on him once upon a time and it stuck. It was also a very apt description of the man's mood, which was constantly dark and stormy. The big man stepped through the saloon doors like a man with nothing to lose. His spurs slapped wood as he sauntered onto the elevated sidewalk that connected all of the buildings on the block. Dressed more immaculately than most in town, Black Bart Horrigan kept his face smoothly shaved, except for the neatly trimmed pencil-thin mustache that framed his upper lip.

With a toothpick clinched tightly between his teeth, Horrigan chuckled. The sound was enough to send even the bravest of men scurrying for cover.

All save Fallon.

The Marshal pushed himself off of the dusty path the townsfolk called a road and patted away the dirt from his clothes.

Unlike the marshal or the men and women who jockeyed for a good spot to watch what was about to happen, Horrigan's clothes were spotless. Dressed in dark colors with a gold inlaid vest, it wasn't hard to believe that the man fancied himself a hero of the west.

"I warned you, Fallon," he said, taking a moment to let each word sink in. "I gave you every opportunity to pull up stakes and ride right on out of town." He wiggled the toothpick around as if fishing for a stray piece of egg from his morning breakfast.

"Horrigan…" the marshal said weakly as he tried to walk away on rubbery legs.

Horrigan stepped into the street, a beefy hand resting easily on the hilt of the chrome-plated pistol resting in the holster on his hip. "I guess some folk just got ta learn the hard way, huh?"

Several paces away, the lawman likewise let his hand fall to the gun on his belt.

The street cleared, the denizens of Broken Eagle seeking shelter from the safety of the buildings lining Main Street. Everyone knew what was coming next.

Showdown.

"I'm warning you, Horrigan," Fallon said.

The big man laughed, squinting against the glare. Only the shadow from his ten-gallon hat shaded his eyes from the hot Arizona sun.

Without a hat of his own, Marshal Fallon's eyes watered. He tried to hide his nervousness, but he wasn't sure he could actually win against a man of Horrigan's skill. Sweat began to run down his face, dripping into his eyes. He could taste the saltiness of it on his chapped lips. He did not like the idea of dying in the middle of a dirt street in some lawless town.

Horrigan sneered.

"Draw," he growled.

As one, both gunfighters pulled their pistols and fired. Puffs of gray gunpowder smoke rose from the muzzle of each gun simultaneously.

Smiling, Horrigan twirled his gun around on his finger before spinning it easily back into its holster.

At the far end of the street, the lawman twitched and clutched at his blood-covered chest before dropping face first to the ground in a lifeless heap.

"Can't say I didn't warn him," Horrigan joked, picking at his teeth with the toothpick.

He flicked the toothpick in the direction of his fallen enemy. "You should've left when ya had the chance, Marshal."

No one cried over the death of Marshal Fallon. In a town like Broken Eagle, being a lawman was a lonely profession, and a short one.

"Too late now, I reckon," Horrigan said with a laugh.

Terrance Mallory watched the entire incident play out in awe.

No sooner had the marshal's body hit the ground when the town *lowlies*, the dregs of society who had nothing-- no home, no food, and no prospects for anything better to come along-- run from their hiding places to swarm over the body like vultures descending on fresh meat. They picked through his pockets and stripped away his clothes, boots, guns, and whatever else he had on him.

"The belt's mine!" one shouted.

"Dem's is some purty boots!" another said, scrambling to get them off the dead man's feet before someone else could get to them first.

"You boys know what I want," Horrigan said as he strode closer to inspect his handiwork.

"Yes, sir, boss," one of the lowlies said even as he tossed the marshal's badge to Horrigan, who plucked it easily from the air.

"Now ain't this a kick? Looks like I'm the new law around here now, boys!" Horrigan proclaimed proudly to a stream of hoots and hollers from the denizens of Broken Eagle.

Was this a trophy to commemorate his win? Perhaps. As a businessman, Mallory understood the gesture. How many times had he likewise taken a trophy from those who had fallen before him? Although he didn't normally use a gun to settle his disagreements, Mallory was no less ruthless in his chosen field.

Horrigan stared proudly at the memento of his victory.

"Nice shootin', mister," Mallory said, breaking the moment as he stepped forward.

"And just who might you be, mister?"

"We've only just arrived in town, sir. I take it you are the sheriff round these parts?"

"Well, we don't take kindly to strangers here, mister. So, what is your business in Broken Eagle--

He smiled and Mallory felt his breath catch.

--stranger?"

"My name is Terrance Mallory, Sheriff. I'm in the-- ah-- procurement business."

Horrigan looked the three strangers over. Although they were dressed the part, he could tell these were no ordinary cowboys. Not only were they far too clean to have been riding the trails for long, their hair was neat and all had shaved recently. Each man carried two pistols, one strapped to each hip.

Buffing his newly acquired badge with a handkerchief pulled from his breast pocket, he offered a sinister smile. "Name's Horrigan. William Horrigan. I run this place. You want to do business here, then you talk to me before you procure anything." The smile widened as he clipped the marshal's badge to his vest. "Am I understood?"

Mallory shook his head. "Yes, sir. We're on our way out to California and are only passing through, but thought your town looked like a nice friendly place to rest up for a few days." He offered a smile of his own to mimic Black Bart's own as he pulled a wad of bills from his pocket. "Maybe do a little business," he added, baiting the hook.

"I see," Horrigan said.

"Maybe play a little poker…"

"You're in luck. That's our second favorite pastime in Broken Eagle."

"What's the first?" one of Mallory's companion's asked.

Horrigan chuckled.

As if remembering that they were there, Mallory motioned toward the men at his side. Both were younger than their boss. "These are my associates. Tim Conrad. Martin Seltz."

"A pleasure, sir," Seltz said, offering a tip of his hat.

Conrad simply said, "Howdy."

Not one to trifle with pleasantries, especially with the hired help, Horrigan ignored the younger men. He chucked a thumb over his shoulder to the *Wild Bill Saloon* and hotel behind him. "Mr. Mallory, if you and your young friends are looking for a good game, this is the place. It's my establishment-- The Wild Bill Saloon. We also rent rooms by the week, the day," he cast a devilish look toward Mallory's men. "And by the hour," he added, taking some grim satisfaction in watching the one named Seltz blush.

From the outside, the Wild Bill Saloon appeared to be a magnificent place, but seeing some of the local working girls hanging out the windows and waving to the new arrivals told Mallory it was most likely a den of debauchery on the inside, as well as a watering hole. Fortunately, that was his kind of place.

"I'm obliged to you, sir," a smiling Mallory said. "I think that'll do just fine."

"You'll find this a right hospitable town, gentlemen," Horrigan offered as he motioned them up the steps to the saloon's swinging door. "Provided you stay on the right side of the law."

"Sounds reasonable," Mallory offered.

"And if there's one thing you'd do well to remember, Mr. Mallory," Horrigan added. "In Broken Eagle I am the law."

"Well, well, well… will you look at that?"

Terrance Mallory and his associates stood in the room they had rented for the night. As he had suspected, the room was greatly overpriced, but then again everything on this trip had amounted to a small fortune.

And worth every penny, he decided. Mallory checked out something from the window, his eye pressed delicately against a telescope. "What did I tell you, boys? This is perfect. Just perfect."

"You really think we can pull this off?" Conrad asked. A slight quiver in his voice betrayed his concern.

"Trust me. Things will work out exactly as advertised," Terrance said. He put on his hat and tossed his associates a conspiratorial wink. He held up a roll of cash. "But first, I have to go and talk with the town's new 'marshal', boys. You two go have some fun. Just watch your backs and I'll see you at dawn."

Leaving the associates to their own devices, Mallory stopped at the top of the staircase, leaned against the railing and watched the people below. The Wild Bill Saloon was everything he had pictured and more. Men played cards at several tables, cigar smoke hovering over them like a cloud. A young piano player tickled the ivories in the far corner, all but oblivious to the two working girls fawning over him. All around the room, girls in fluffy dresses and corsets flittered about the room in search of their next mark. At the bar, a grizzled man with a stark white beard kept the booze flowing.

"Now this…" he said proudly. "This is my kind of place!"

Still smiling, Terrance made his way down the stairs to the saloon floor, taking it all in and enjoying every minute of it. He tipped his hat to a pair of dancing ladies as he passed. They giggled like schoolgirls, which made him happy. He felt all eyes on him, but he didn't care.

At a nearby table, William Horrigan is busy playing cards.

Terrance pulled a cigar from his shirt pocket before changing course to head in that direction. "I think you're bluffing, Clem," he heard the man say as he got closer.

"Well, it's gon' cost ya ta find out," the man named Clem said. He smiled around the unlit fat cigar chomped between his brown teeth.

"Then let's see what you've…"

Mallory took a seat at the table's lone empty chair without an invite and allowed one of the working girls to light his cigar.

"You know, Mr. Mallory, we might all be friends here, but newcomers are not always welcome at the playing table," Horrigan said without turning to face the newcomer. His eyes never left the opponent sitting across the table from him as he lays down his cards and winning the hand.

Horrigan turned to look at Mallory. "Impolite newcomers are welcome even less," he added, the threat evidenced in his stare.

Ignoring the threat, Mallory unrolled a wad of one hundred-dollar bills.

"That's a shame," Mallory said as he tossed some cash into the pot. "Deal me in."

Horrigan studied the newcomer. "You know, I can't tell if you're trying to con me or not, Mr. Mallory."

"You'll have to ante up to find out."

Horrigan chuckled and tossed out the first card in the deal.

"I guess we'll just have to deal you in, then."

The morning sun rose over the mountains to the east of the small town of Broken Eagle. From some hidden perch, a rooster crowed, alerting the earlier risers that dawn had arrived.

Horrigan stepped out of the saloon, flanked by several of his men. Despite having only a few short hours to catch some sleep after the poker game, the men were ready to face the challenge ahead. "Time?" Horrigan asked, not bothering to fish out his newly won pocket watch.

"Quarter of, boss," one of the lackeys said.

A shrill whistle split the early morning air.

Horrigan smiled.

"Right on time."

The 6:10 train from Tucson made a brief stop in Broken Eagle twice a week, once on the way to New Mexico, and again on the return trip. If not for the tiny depot station, Broken Eagle probably would have dried up and been reclaimed by the desert years earlier. For a less than reputable businessman like William Horrigan, the depot was an invaluable resource. His contacts on the train had been paid a pretty penny to smuggle in a shipment for him, shipped under the guise of mining supplies. They had no idea what was really inside the crates, however, and they were all far too smart to think about crossing Horrigan. His reputation preceded him. Horrigan has planned this caper to perfection for quite some time.

Nothing would go wrong.

"What a beautiful day to meet a train, eh, gentlemen?" he said as he mounted his horse.

"Yeah it is, boss. Yeah it is."

"We do this quick, quiet, and clean. Just like we planned," he told his men. "You know what to do, boys, so let's get it done."

"Sheriff!"

Horrigan turned to face the lowlie running toward him. He hated having to deal with the dregs. They smelled, but they had their uses. "That's *Marshal*," he said. "Marshal Horrigan."

"Right. Sorry, boss."

Horrigan sighed.

"Marshal, you remember them strangers you asked me ta check in on?"

"Yeah?"

"They're gone, boss! Nobody's seen 'em all morning!"

"Waddaya mean, nobody's seen 'em? Where'd they go then?" he shouted. Before he could say anything more, the train whistle once again cut through the still morning air. "No. They couldn't be… could they?" Horrigan muttered. "Could they be here for the train?"

"What's that, boss?"

"Oh no. They're after my train."

"Sure ain't much to look at, is it?" Martin Seltz commented.

"I don't know, boys," Terrance Mallory said. "Looks like a couple million in gold to me."

Perched on top of a cliff looking down at the train depot below them, the three men waited. Below, the depot for Broken Eagle sat surrounded by dirt. In fact, calling it a depot was generous. It was little more than a small shack and platform for loading and unloading sitting next to train tracks in the middle of nowhere, not even close to town. It had taken Mallory and his boys about twenty minutes on horseback to reach it.

"Terrance, the train's a'comin!" Tim Conrad shouts, pointing with glee toward the plume of smoke shooting into the air from a small speck just visible on the horizon.

"Time to ride, boys!" Mallory pulled himself into the saddle of his horse. They had *borrowed* three steeds from the stables before dawn. He spurred the horse and it leapt into motion, heading straight toward the depot.

Conrad followed suit, adding a hooting "Giddeyup!"

Martin Seltz hopped in the small carriage tied behind a team of two horses, prodded them into motion, and followed his companions.

The three men made their way down the dusty slope, kicking up dirt in their wake. It only took a few moments to reach the depot. The train was closer now and coming in at full speed. Martin Seltz leapt onto the platform and rubbed his hands together.

"Oh boy, we're going to be rich!" he shouted.

"Ah wouldn't be too sure of that if I was you, Mr. Seltz," a familiar voice said calmly.

The three newcomers spun at the sound just in time to see the last person they expected step onto the platform. In his hand, he held an ivory-handled six-shooter. The hammer was cocked and aimed squarely at Terrance Mallory. His men stood in the dirt and watched the standoff, their hands resting on the guns holstered at their hip.

"Horrigan!" Conrad shouted.

"How did he…" Seltz started, but a gesture from his boss silenced him.

Mallory held his hands out to his sides, making sure not to stray anywhere near the pistols holstered on his hip. "We don't want any trouble," he said calmly. "We just want the train."

Horrigan lifted the gun higher. "Then we have a problem, gentlemen. You see, that train out there?" He pointed with his free hand. "It's mine."

"Yours?"

"Yes." Horrigan said. "Mine. And I don't take too kindly to thieves trying to take what's mine."

"Maybe we can make a deal," Mallory said. He hoped that talking could help. If the outlaw were willing to bargain long enough to keep from getting shot, it would give him time to come up with a plan.

Sadly, the outlaw had other plans.

"I don't deal," Horrigan said.

"Somehow, I knew you were going to say that," Mallory said.

"Every dog has his day, Mr. Mallory," Horrigan said, his finger tightening on the trigger. "I'm afraid today ain't yours. Game over. You lose."

Terrance Mallory closed his eyes and awaited the inevitable, but a startled shout from Tim Conrad snapped him back to the moment.

"We have another problem, guys! We've got company!"

Horrigan's gaze followed along the invisible line from the young thief's finger toward the last thing he had ever expected to see again in his life. The look on his face was one that Mallory hadn't noticed since they arrived at Broken Eagle.

It was fear.

"Horrigan, what is this?" Mallory demanded. "Is this part of the... Who are those guys?"

"Oh hell," Horrigan muttered. "We're in trouble."

"What kind of trouble?"

"We've got to get out of here," Horrigan demanded. "Now!"

"What the hell are you talking about, man?" Mallory shouted. "I paid good--"

It was clear that the man called Horrigan wasn't listening. Gun at his side, he stared at the three men approaching the depot from the area that Mallory recalled was marked as a canyon on the map he'd studied before they arrived.

"It's impossible," Horrigan said. "It... it can't be them!"

"Can't be who?" Mallory demanded. "Dammit, Horrigan! Who?"

"It's the Glutch Brothers," the outlaw finally said, but all trace of his accent vanished.

"What's so special about..." Mallory started, but then he got a good look at the men coming their way.

There were three of them, each easily six foot, five inches or more. They wore long dusters that scraped along the dusty earth. Each was armed with pistols similar to the ones everyone on the platform carried. They certainly looked like the kind of cowboys Mallory had heard about, rough and tumble men who had lived out in the wild so long that they no longer lived by the same conventional rules as the rest of society. Even men like William Horrigan, for all their professed villainy, were simply playing their parts. Their ten-gallon cowboy hats were dirty and frayed, faded from many days in the harsh desert sun. Clouds of dust rose behind them with each heavy thick-booted footfall.

"Oh my God," Mallory breathed.

Horrigan looked as though he might faint. "It's the Glutch Brothers," he repeated.

"What's wrong with their faces?" Conrad asked as they reached the platform.

The Glutch Brothers reached the platform in synch, leaping from the hard-packed desert sand to the platform where they towered over everyone else.

Their sun-baked skin was rough as shoe leather and mottled from abuse and long days in the intense desert sun. They almost look like dead men. From a distance, they had looked like men who had spent to much time in the sun, but now that they were close enough to touch, Mallory knew them for exactly what they were.

"'morning, gents," the lead brother said.

"The Glutch Brothers," Horrigan repeated. "They're bad news."

"They're robots," Martin Seltz shouted.

"No," Mallory said. "It's worse than that."

"We're dead," Horrigan added.

PART 2: WHAT IS...

THE ALERT CLAXON BLARED.

It's shrill, high-pitched warble filling every corner and corridor, the alarm was impossible to ignore. Emergency alert signals flashed wildly across computer screens inside the very high tech control room where men and women scrambled to isolate and fix the problem that triggered the alarm in the first place.

"What the hell is going on?" Ivan Brown, the technical director of Showdown at Broken Eagle Amusement Services shouted as he entered the room. "Somebody report!"

His answer came only as a cacophony of alarms mixed with murmured voices.

Brown, a tall, thin man with thinning hair that was starting to gray around the edges, leaned over a female technician. "What have you got, Rimza?"

He was hoping for good news.

He was going to be disappointed.

"I haven't locked down the details yet, but it's not good news," she said.

Before her supervisor could question that, there came a shout from across the room that somehow cut through the din. "I've got activity on the transport disk!" Technician Anderson yelled. "Alcove two!" He pointed to the alcove, even though everyone there was familiar with it. Crackles of electricity arced within the metal and plastic frame.

"Who is it!?" Brown demanded as arcs of energy began to coalesce into a fairly human shape. "Who the hell is it?"

The energy ball expands and takes on the proportions of a man then suddenly, Marshal James Fallon, the lawman who had been fatally shot by William Horrigan in Broken Eagle earlier, is standing on the pad. The marshal was still wearing the same clothes he had been wearing on the streets of Broken Eagle, but now they were caked with blood from where he had been shot.

"Marshal Fallon?" Brown shouted. He runs over to the marshal as gravity takes over and the wounded man drops to the floor like a stone. Supervisor Brown managed to catch the lawman before his head can hit the metal casing.

"Chris?" he shouted to the man, calling him by his true first name. "Chris, can you hear me?"

"This isn't right," one of the technicians said, his voice on the verge of breaking. "What's wrong with him?"

"Get me a medic!" Brown ordered.

"It's too late," Rimza whispered, her fingers pressed against the man's neck. "He's dead, sir. I'm sorry."

Brown pulled his hand away from the wound, surprised to see real blood there. The bullet wounds were real.

"How the hell did that happen?" another tech shouted. "How did live rounds get inside the scenario?"

"Turn that damn alarm off," Brown said, getting to his feet as a medical team burst into the room.

The blaring alert claxon silenced, dropping the room into eerie silence. In all the time he had worked there, Ivan Brown had never heard this room so quiet.

"What happened in there?" he asked. It was such a simple question--

--that had no simple answer.

Nearby, one of the technicians at a work console shouted over the alarms as sparks exploded from her neighbor's console, knocking another tech to the ground.

Trying to ignore the chaos erupting around them, Brown leaned over Rimza's shoulder and examined her findings on the computer screen. He can't believe what he's seeing. "A breach?" he asked. "Are you sure?"

"Yes, sir."

"How's that possible?"

"Someone hacked into our central core."

Brown cannot believe it. "But Broken Eagle is unbreachable!"

The technician tried to pull up data on the computer, but the corrupted data won't comply.

"Apparently not, sir! Somebody got in."

"Who?" Brown asked, his anger having reached its limit.

"I don't know."

"Find out who did this and how. And do it now."

"Offhand, I'd guess it was them," Rimza said, pointing toward one of the still functioning screens. He followed her line and turned to face the screen, the look on his face betraying his fear. Despite all her years as a technician, Rimza had never seen anything like it before.

Unfortunately, Ivan Brown had.

"My God," he whispered as soon as he saw it.

"Who are they?" Rimza asked.

"Those are the Glutch Brothers."

"The who?"

"The Glutch Brothers."

"They don't look human."

"They're not."

"Are they…" Rimza gasped, her voice trailing off as the complete picture formed in her mind. "Th--they're cyborgs!"

"It's worse than that," Brown said. "Much worse."

"How could things be worse?"

On the screen, they watched as the Glutch Brothers stepped onto the platform like men on a mission as weathered boards creaked under their combined weight. They stopped before their clients: Terrance Mallory, Tim Conrad, and Martin Seltz. William Horrigan was also on the platform. To call the Glutch's scary looking was an understatement. With their mechanical implants showing, including one of them with a glowing red bulb where an eye should have been. They towered over the others, standing easily seven feet tall and larger than life.

"The Glutch Brothers are animatronic robots. They were part of a failed experiment a decade or so back. They were designed to interact with authenticity to the park's visitors in a way that the management at the time did not thing that human actors could. The Glutch family was one of several dozen groups that were programmed to believe they were living in the old west. It was successful for a time."

"I remember hearing stories about that," Rimza said. "Why was it shut down?"

"The robots proved violently unstable and the project was scrapped. I was informed that all of them had been destroyed twenty some odd years ago, but I guess they missed these three.

"What do you think they want?"

Brown leaned heavily on the console to steady his nerves. Although he hadn't witnessed it firsthand, he had been made aware of the problems that led to the robotics program being dismantled. "I don't know. They were originally part of the wild west scenario that's currently running. Perhaps they've just reverted to their original programming. If that's the case, then they should still think they're cowboys and everything will be okay."

"Do you really believe that, Director?"

"No," Brown said. "No, I Do not."

"I was afraid you were going to say that," Rimza muttered. "So, what do we do?"

"First, we need to get that program off-line and get those people out of there."

"How?"

"Get Mitchell on the phone. Tell him we have a code red."

The heat in Broken Eagle was intolerable.

This was by design, of course. Until the arrival of the creatures from a nightmare, Terrance Mallory appreciated that attention to detail. Now that this was no longer a game, he felt sweat roll down his back as he and his companions each took a step back as the new arrivals stepped onto the platform in front of them. The Glutch brothers walked at their own pace, slow and deliberate, as if they haven't a care in the world. They don't seem to be in any hurry.

"Uh, Horrigan, you want to explain to me why there are robots in this Wild West program of yours? We paid for a true Wild West experience. We didn't pay for freakin' robots!"

Horrigan looked as though he were about to go into a full-blown panic attack. "I wish I could," he stammered. "All I know is they shouldn't be here!"

"Get a grip, man!" Mallory said, but Horrigan wasn't listening.

The new sheriff of Broken Eagle pulled his second six-shooter from its holster, pointed them in the direction of the Glutch Brothers, and opened fire, two shots from each.

They had no effect.

The robotic cowboys lumbered forward.

Terrance grabbed Horrigan by the shoulder and pulled him away from the approaching robotic cowboys, shouting that they had to leave, but Horrigan wasn't listening. He squeezed off two more shots.

"We have to get out of here!" Mallory shouted, tugging at Horrigan. "Let's go!"

As though chased by the devil himself, the four men ran back the way they had come, leaping from the platform to the dusty desert sand below. They made a beeline toward the hill that Terrance and his boys had come down earlier at a full run.

On the platform, the Glutch Brothers watch them leave.

Darryl Glutch cawed excitedly.

"You're gonna bust a gut, brother," Tommy Glutch said.

"Lookit them varmints run!" Darryl shouted, his voice still filled with static.

"You want I should go after them, Hoss?" Wayne Glutch asked. He was the brothers' cousin. A natural born tracker, Wayne was also as strong as an ox. That had come in handy during many a dust up at The Wild Bill Saloon on a Saturday night. A couple belts of the good stuff ol' Mary Lou kept under the bar and Wayne was ten feet tall, bulletproof, and ready to fight any man who looked at him so much as sideways.

Tommy Glutch spit a wad of tobacco on the ground. "Naw," he said after wiping the back of his hand across his mouth. "Let 'em go. We got ourselves a train to catch."

Terrance Mallory watched the Glutch Brothers through the telescope.

"Well, gentlemen, this is not good," he said once he rejoined them on the opposite side of the rocky outcropping they were using for shelter.

"What did you see?" Tim Conrad asked.

"They aren't coming after us," Mallory said. "At least not yet."

"That's good news, right?" Martin Seltz asked.

"Maybe. I really don't know," Mallory said. He turned a hard stare toward Horrigan. "This isn't exactly what I signed us up for."

"Why are you looking at me," Horrigan said. "I just work here. I'm not a real cowboy. I'm an actor."

"So, I've noticed," Seltz remarked.

"Right now, the best thing we can do is keep our wits about us," Mallory said. "For all we know this is some wild new play the people in charge have thrown at us to keep us on our toes. I'm not happy about it, but it is what it is."

"And if it's not part of the scenario?"

"Well, Tim, I'd like to think they would send somebody in here to get us then. Either way, I think the best thing we can do right now is keep an eye on the Glutch Brothers and stay out of their way."

"And what if they have other plans?" Seltz asked.

"Then we plan for that too."

"What are they doing down there, Mallory?" Horrigan asked.

Mallory chanced another look through the lens. "Looks like they're waiting on the train. Same as us. What I want to know is why?"

"What possible interest could these robot rejects want with the train?" Conrad asked. "It's just a prop, isn't it? Not real gold."

Horrigan nodded.

Mallory grabbed Horrigan by the shirt and hauled him to his feet. Angry, he looked the actor directly in the eyes. "I want to know what is going on, Horrigan, so you'd better start talking or be prepared to lose some teeth."

"How am I supposed to know?" Horrigan shouted, his voice on the verge of breaking.

"This is your town, isn't it?"

"Look, man, I'm an actor. This is just a job. I'm telling you, I don't know what this is."

"The brochure never mentioned anything like this," Mallory said. "Is this some new variation to test us or something?"

"We are so past the brochure."

"What the hell does that mean?"

On the verge of panic, Horrigan shouted at Terrance Mallory. "Hey! This isn't exactly what I signed on for either, pal!" He pointed wildly toward the depot area. "And they sure as hell aren't supposed to be here either!"

"Then there has to be some kind of malfunction," Tim interrupted. "That's the only thing that makes sense." He turned to Horrigan. "Do you know where these things have been stored?"

"No idea."

"Okay. How about fail safes? Are there any overrides in place that will allow us to cancel the program from inside?"

"No," the faux cowboy said. "At least not in here. The control complex is supposed to be monitoring the game from up there." He pointed toward the clear blue sky above their head. "They're supposed to shut down the program if things get out of hand."

"Then, why haven't they?" Conrad said, asking the question they've all been thinking.

"That's a damned good question, Tim," Mallory said. "Something's wrong up there.

"It's not exactly sunshine and roses down here either, boss," Seltz reminded him.

Horrigan snapped back into his Black Bart character's attitude. "Maybe it is all part of the game. Did you ever think of that? Maybe it's something new they've added to spice things up. I mean, they were after the train too. Like you said, it's only a game!

Horrigan popped a fresh toothpick into his mouth. Seemingly no longer afraid, the actor had found security in his character's arrogance. "What I don't get," he offered. "Is what a group of robots would want with a train filled with bars of fake gold?

Mallory smiled. "They wouldn't." He snapped his fingers. "That's it! Don't you see? They actually think they're still the Glutch Brothers."

"I don't follow," Conrad said.

"Their programming isn't faulty," Mallory explained. "They still think this is their town. If you came home and found someone living in your house, what would you do?"

"I'd run them out," Conrad said.

"I think that's what we're dealing with here?"

"How can you be sure, boss?"

"I can't." Mallory said. "This is all guess work, but it makes sense. Wherever they've been all this time, wherever the company has had them stored, somehow these things were reactivated and they came home to find a whole new group of people living in their homes."

He pulled his pistol and checked the bullets in his six-shooter to make sure he had a full clip. Like Horrigan, Mallory was slipping back into character as the tough stranger riding into town.

"Them things is full of blanks, remember," Horrigan warned.

"I know that," Mallory said. "We all know that, but they don't know that." He chucked a thumb in the direction of the robots waiting patiently for the train to arrive. "If their programming is still active and they think this is real then these bullets should affect them just like the real thing."

"I hear a lot of maybes in there," Horrigan said. "What if you're wrong?"

"Then I'm wrong," Mallory said.

"That's not very reassuring," Seltz said.

Mallory barked a laugh.

"So, what's the plan, boss?" Conrad asked.

Mallory snapped the barrel closed on his gun and slipped it with practiced ease back into its holster. "I say we go down there and ask them what's going on."

"Are you insane?" Horrigan said.

"If they think it's all just a game…" Mallory said. "Well, I guess it's up to us to show them the error of their ways.

Horrigan shook his head.

"We're all gonna die," he muttered.

PART 3: WHAT WILL BE...

IN THE SHOWDOWN AT BROKEN EAGLE CONTROL ROOM, SUPERVISOR Ivan Brown hoped Plan B would work. While talking with the technician in charge of transport control, he offered a silent prayer, something he hadn't done since he'd been a little boy afraid of the dark and praying for someone to keep the monsters under the bed while he slept.

If only he could dispatch the monsters inside his theme park so easily.

"Can we lock on to any of the actors or the clients and beam them out of there like we did with Chris?" he asked. A wave of sadness tugged at him at the thought of his dead friend who had played the role of Marshal Fallon. They had known one another for years. He pushed the memories away. There would be time to mourn his friend later, after they saved everyone else still trapped inside.

"No, sir. Not at present."

"And the emergency overrides still aren't working on the doors?"

"I'm afraid not," Technician Rimza said.

"Damn," Brown muttered. "Okay. We go with the tactical option." He plucked a red phone from the workstation. He did not have to dial a number. "Mr. Mitchell, you have a go! Have your men assembled and ready for insertion in five minutes."

"Copy that," the voice on the other end said before disconnecting the call.

"Uh, we may not have five minutes, Mr. Brown," Rimza said.

"What's wrong now?" Brown asked, returning to her terminal.

"See for yourself." Pointing to the screen, she noted that Horrigan, Mallory, and the others were making their way back down the hill toward the depot where the robotic Glutch Brothers waited. "Looks like somebody decided to do something stupid."

"Are they insane? Those fools are going to get themselves killed."

"Mitchell!" Brown shouted into the red phone. "Deploy your team now!"

Commander Mitchell and his squad of trained combat soldiers took position outside of one of the many service access doors into the Broken Eagle program. Whatever malfunction had caused the robot actors to go haywire had also sealed the doors. One of the operations technicians was working on the problem. Each member of his team was decked out in full body armor and they carried high-powered weaponry. He was confident that his people could handle whatever situation they encountered once they got inside, a process that was taking far longer than he'd have liked.

"Status, Mr. Reynolds?" he asked the technician, pacing back and forth behind the man as he worked inside the open access panel.

"I'm working on it," Reynolds said through grit teeth.

"Work faster."

"Work faster," Reynolds parroted. "Oh, sure. Like it's that easy."

"What was that?"

"Nothing."

With a loud metal on metal scrape, the door's automatic lock released and the door slid open a crack. Just beyond was the soundstage where Broken Eagle existed.

"Great job, Reynolds. Step back," Mitchell said. He clicked the radio microphone clipped to his shoulder. "Control, we are ready to go on your word."

"You have a go," came Supervisor Brown's anxious reply.

Mitchell stepped in front of the door. "Listen up, ladies and gentlemen. Here's the situation. Due to some unexplained mechanical breach or malfunction, three of the animatronic actors that were part of the original design have been reanimated and have somehow been reintegrated into the program. We have clients and actors trapped inside and in imminent danger. Once inside we'll hitch a ride on the train that'll take us right to our targets. Once we've engaged, the mechanical units are to be terminated immediately. We're not taking any chances so Rodriguez will stay on station here to watch the door until our return. This is the only way in or out of Broken Eagle. If anything goes wrong, this is our fall back point. Any questions? No. Good. Everybody ready?"

A chorus of affirmatives answered.

"Do it," he told Reynolds, whose men stood at the door to manually pull it open.

The access door slid open slowly under manual power, offering a desert view and a blast of dry, desert air. Mitchell immediately felt sweat dripping down his back as he stepped across the threshold into the Broken Eagle simulation. The interior of the door, he noted, was painted to look like mountain vistas in the distance under a powder blue sky, all part of the simulation's backdrop.

"Watch yourselves, folks," he said once they were inside. "We're entering the Twilight Zone."

Mitchell stopped next to a set of railroad tracks. He could hear the train approaching and knows, based on the schematics he studied, that the train runs along a track near the outer backdrop wall until it reaches a point where it heads into the simulation. The plan he devised would have his assault troop hitch a ride on the train into Broken Eagle so they can surprise the Glutch Brother robots, who are apparently planning to rob the train.

"We're inside, Control," Mitchell reports. "I need an ETA on the train."

No answer.

"Control, are you there?"

"Sir?" one of the soldiers asked.

"Anyone else getting a signal?" Mitchell asked. He was rewarded by several shaking heads and irritated looks. Something has disrupted transmissions from the control room or has blocked them inside the program. That makes him nervous. "Say again, Control," he repeated. "There's some kind of interference. I can't make out your last transmission. I need an estimated time or arrival on the…"

Mitchell's voice caught in his throat as he saw the train approaching at top speed. Lifting the faceplate on his helmet for a better look, his eyes grow wide with shock at the sight coming toward him. An experienced soldier, Mitchell's service record read like a fiction novel, even though every entry was absolute truth. However, what he saw on that train made his blood run cold and his knees go weak.

The train screamed past with a warble of its whistle screaming into the summer heat.

Mitchell and his team watched with awe, but none of them attempted to hop on board the train. He toggled the mic on his shoulder and hoped the signal was strong enough to cut through.

"Control, we have a serious problem down here."

"Brothers, the train's a'coming."

On the platform of the Broken Eagle train depot, the Glutch Brothers smiled as they watched the train approach. Tommy Glutch slapped his companions on the shoulders. "This is it, boys. This here's our ticket to getting back our homes."

"This is gonna be good," Darryl Glutch said.

Not far away, Terrance Mallory peeked around the edge of the depot at the approaching train and the three Glutch Brothers waiting for it. So far, they hadn't noticed him, or if they had, they did not seem to care. No matter which, he wasn't going to question his good fortune. He and the others were originally supposed to fight Horrigan and his men for the train. That was the goal of the Showdown at Broken Eagle scenario he'd paid for. Robots had not been on the menu, but regardless of how or why they were there, the Glutch Brothers had become part of the game.

It was a game that Terrance Mallory still very much planned to win.

"They're still there," he whispered to his companions as they hugged the depot's far wall. "I guess they're waiting on…"

The train whistle interrupted his thought.

Horrigan slid in close to Mallory. He pointed in the direction of the platform with his gun. "Is that…?"

"Yep. train's coming in," Mallory said. "And we can't let them take it."

"And just how do you propose we stop them?"

"Follow me." Gun in hand, he stepped softly onto the platform, careful not to make a sound as he moved into position behind the Glutch Brothers.

The train's horn signaled its arrival as it slowed and coasted into the depot.

Mallory pulled back the hammer on his pistol.

The Glutch Brothers turned in unison at the sound and stood face to face with Terrance Mallory. "Howdy, boys," Mallory said.

Tommy Glutch stepped forward, his single red eye glowing under the shade of the depot roof. "You sure you wanna do that, hombre?" he asked. "It's far too purty a day f'r me to have to kill someone, so you just back on off now, hear?"

Mallory raised the gun to chest level. "I can't do that. Train's mine. You can't have it."

"Is that so?"

"It is."

Smiling, Tommy Glutch spread his arms wide, palms up so that his opponent could see the guns hanging at his hip. "What are you going to do, pardner, shoot me? 'Cause that's the only way you're gonna get near that train."

"If you say so," Mallory said as he opened fire, unleashing all six bullets in his pistol.

The elder Glutch didn't so much as flinch nor did he feel the impact of a single bullet.

He laughed. "That the best ya'll got?"

And that was when Terrance Mallory realized his mistake.

The robotic cowboys knew the guns weren't real.

The Glutch brother grabbed the stranger's gun hand and squeezed, crushing both the gun and Mallory's hand into an inseparable mass of bone, blood, and steel.

Mallory screamed.

It made no impact on his attacker.

"Don't say I didn't warn ya, hombre."

Tommy Glutch swung out, tossing his enemy toward the depot building.

Terrance Mallory crashed through the depot wall, which was more for looks than actual use so it was made from cheap, thin pressboard, a fact that saved the man's life. He landed inside the small building, crashing hard against the supplies stored there.

Seeing their boss dispatched so cavalierly, Tim Conrad and Martin Seltz jumped onto the depot's platform. Tim took a swing at Tommy Glutch with a wooden post he'd picked up from the wood pile at the side of the building.

Tommy made no move to duck or avoid the attack. Instead, he reached out and grabbed the wooden post, snapping it in two with ease.

"Now that weren't very nice," he said with a hint of playfulness. "Didn't your ma teach you no manners?"

The elder Glutch planted a fist into the younger man's chest and sent him flying backward. Conrad landed hard on his back halfway down the platform. He looked down at his bandaged hand, almost as surprised by his newfound strength than the man he had just thrown across the depot landing.

There was no time to ponder this new discovery, however.

"Die, you bastards!" Seltz shouted as he tried to shoot them down, but his gun also fired blanks as Mallory's had.

The robot seemed to stagger as if hit, but then it looked down and realized that it wasn't being hit. "Well ain't that th' damndest thing?" he said before continuing forward with a look of satisfaction creasing its damaged face.

Seltz turned to run, but the Glutch Brother was faster. He grabbed the man by the arm and jerked him backward, knocking him off balance and pulling him back until he stood face to face with the animatronic cowboy. He tried to speak, but couldn't form the words.

The robot smiled--

--and in one fluid motion snapped Martin Seltz's neck.

Darryl Glutch looked at the lifeless man in his grip for a second as if he unsure of what just happened. If he had been human, it would look as though he perhaps felt a small pang of guilt over killing Martin Seltz.

The moment passed quickly.

Darryl Glutch released his grip and Seltz's corpse dropped to the depot platform in a lifeless heap.

From the corner of the depot, Horrigan watched in horror as the robot easily snapped young Tim Seltz's neck, killing him instantly. That was all the incentive the actor playing the part of William Horrigan needed.

"To hell with this," he muttered. He made a run for it, setting off toward the painted backdrop in search of an exit.

He heard the train's brakes squeal as it came to rest at the depot. He knew better, but Horrigan chanced a look in the train's direction, hoping for just a brief moment that the locomotive was his ticket to freedom. He saw movement inside the train.

Horrigan ran toward the train, arms waving to get someone's attention in the hope that whoever was on the train would rescue him or end the game. He had always heard that there was safety in numbers. He never needed that statement to be more true than today. He allowed himself to relax as he stopped in front of the train. For the first time since the arrival of the Glutch Brothers, he thought he just might make it out alive.

And then he saw who was riding the train.

Horrigan's smile faded, replaced instantly by terror.

He managed not to scream as the first passenger stepped off the locomotive onto the platform.

"Howdy," the new arrival said, tipping his hat.

Much like the Glutch Brothers, the riders on the train were the old robots that had made up the original denizens of Broken Eagle before management had decided to replace them with human actors playing similar roles. Also, like the Glutches, the robots looked as though they had dug themselves out of a grave. Pieces of synthetic skin were missing or hanging from metal bone, but they didn't seem to notice.

The first man off the train had a familiar look. He was dressed almost identically to Horrigan and sported the same Old West style mustache. He had no doubt that this had been the original William Horrigan character.

"Oh, crap," Horrigan whispered, knowing he was about to die.

"We're back, boys!"

Once the train ground to a halt at the Broken Eagle Depot, the robotic passengers disembarked. The riders ranged from simple prospectors to gun fighters, farmers to your average cowboy straight out of a movie. Some were rowdy, but others seemed more refined and gentlemanly.

The Glutch Brothers waited for them on the platform.

"Glad you fellers could make it," Tommy Glutch said.

One of the robots, a well-dressed man in a suit, tie, and clean hat, walked toward him while biting off the end of a cigar. "Excellent job, boys," he said. "Damned fine work."

"Always happy to help, boss," Tommy Glutch said as he struck a match and held it out to the new arrival. The refined robot bowed slightly toward the match. The boss puffed three times to light it.

"Any problems?" the boss asked.

"Nothin' we couldn't handle," Darryl said.

"Howdy, boys," a familiar voice called. The Glutch Brothers turned to see their Pa, Jedediah Glutch hobble off the train, a cane in one hand to help with his balance. His crushed leg scrapped along behind him.

"You okay, Pa?"

"Right as rain, boys," he said with a smile. "Ol' Doc Pritchert says he'll have me fixed up in no time once we get back to his office."

"All right, boys," the boss said. "What say we take back our town and get your pappy some medicine?"

"I'd say that sound about like a plan," Tommy Glutch said. "Wayne, Darryl, you take a couple of the boys and finish up with these bozos and we'll take care of Broken Eagle."

"With pleasure," Cousin Wayne said. "I'll be home in time for supper."

"Let's go," Darryl said.

While the town's original inhabitants marched toward Broken Eagle, Wayne and three of his pals headed across the platform. Darryl pushed his way through the hole in the wall made when the stranger had been thrown through it earlier.

The stranger lay there, his arm and leg each twisted around in unnatural directions. He was conscious, but in too much pain to be much of a threat.

"Well, lookee here," Darryl said. "I guess you picked the wrong town to steal, didn't you, partner?"

"We just wanted to play the game," Terrance Mallory croaked though the pain.

"This is my life, stranger. It ain't no game."

"You don't have to kill me."

Darryl Glutch smiled. "No, but I'm going to anyway," he said and started toward the injured stranger. Before he made it two steps he heard the floorboards creak. He spun in the direction of the sound.

"Who's there?" he demanded.

In the corner stood another stranger. He held a large contraption in his hand unlike anything Darryl Glutch had ever seen before in his life.

"Hi there," the stranger said.

"An' just whut th' hell are..." Darryl started.

Commander Mitchell opened fire with the heavy assault weapon in his grip.

Unlike those actors and clients inserted into the Showdown at Broken Eagle program, he wasn't carrying blanks. The weapon's kick echoed through the small room.

Caught completely off guard, Darryl Glutch was blown through the wall on impact. The Glutch Brother hit the desert floor, kicking up a plume of dust. He did not move, a sizzling hole where his chest had been only seconds earlier.

Mitchell exited the storeroom and looked down at the unmoving robotic cowboy. "Bye, buckaroo," he said as he clipped the mic on his shoulder. "This is Mitchell. Exit route is secure. Let's get these people out of here," he ordered.

"Copy that," a voice replied in his ear.

"Now that..." Darryl Glutch said as he pushed himself up from the ground. Despite the large hole in his chest, somehow the robot continued to function, albeit at a diminished level. "--hurt," he said once he was back on his feet.

Surprised by the resilience of the robot cowboy, Mitchell wondered if it was possible to actually destroy them. Fortunately, that wasn't his directive. "Fall back," he called into the mic. "We've got to go! Now!"

Mitchell's troops led the surviving actors and clients, including the severely injured Terrance Mallory and a frightened William Horrigan out of the Broken Eagle toward the horizon where they had secured the emergency exit. Several of the troopers laid down cover fire to hold off the robots that gave chase.

Mitchell was surprised when they stopped following and headed back toward town, but he didn't have time to ponder this new sequence of events. His orders were to get the people out and seal the town. Everything else could be sorted out after they were safe.

"Keep it moving, folks," he told them when they reached the emergency hatch. "Step lively. come on. come on."

Once everyone was through the hatch, Mitchell followed. He was the last one out.

"Seal it up," he ordered the technician, who moved in and started welding the access panel closed. Mitchell breathed a sigh of relief then toggled the mic again. "Mitchell to Command. We've got them."

"Any casualties?"

"I'm afraid so," Mitchell said as Tim Conrad and Terrance Mallory cried over their dead friend.

"Is there any chance of the problem spreading beyond the Broken Eagle perimeter?" Supervisor Brown asked.

"I don't think so. We were not pursued. They seemed more interested in the town than in coming after us. The hatch has been sealed and the perimeter is secured. We may have to content ourselves with permanently sealing off the dome."

"Will that hold them?"

"As long as the robots remain active inside, it is not safe for anyone to enter Broken Eagle. The program will have to be shut down."

"Unless we find another alternative," Brown said, thinking of a back-up strategy. He still had corporate managers to appease and they would not simply pull the plug on a huge investment like Showdown at Broken Eagle.

"I beg your pardon, sir?"

"Nothing," Brown said. "Just thinking out loud. Secure all exits. I'll pass your recommendation up the ladder and see what management wants us to do.

"I can only imagine," Mitchell said.

It was business as usual in Broken Eagle.

As the artificial sun rose against the eastern side of the dome, the robotic cowboys went about their business as if they were the actual cowboys they had been created to imitate.

No longer was Showdown at Broken Eagle a playground for only those few who could afford the elaborate price tag. Now, it was open to the public for a meager entrance fee. And the company was raking in record profits. The families of those injured had been quietly paid off and no one outside of a select few would ever know the truth about what had happened when the Glutch Brothers returned.

No one could explain how the deactivated circuits had restarted or how the simplistic robots had been able to repair themselves, something they were not programmed to do.

Without those answers, the only solution was to seal off the dome that housed the program. No human would ever step foot inside the dome again, unless or until the robots broke down and fell into disrepair. Only then, would they consider sending in a team to clear the town.

Since the robots thought they were real people living in the old west with no desire to stray beyond the confines of Broken Eagle, it was decided to let them go about their lives.

Many on the board of directors for the amusement park speculated that this would ruin the company. They were mistaken.

High above the tiny desert prospect town crowds gathered. Dozens of catwalks and observation rooms, hidden from view to those inside, ringed the dome and were packed to capacity with paying customers eager to get a good look at the ultimate Old West experience.

A tour guide reiterated the history of Broken Eagle and about the robotic recreation that her employer has put together below. It was billed as the closest thing to looking back through time at how real frontier cowboys lived their lives.

The public loved it.

Showdown at Broken Eagle was a bon-a-fide hit.

On the wall by the entrance hung a shiny plastic plaque that told the story of Broken Eagle.

It read:

Showdown at Broken Eagle.

The ultimate time trip museum.

See and experience the past like never before.

The Old West.

An exciting and barbaric time in our nation's history, the booming west was a place where miners, settlers, and frontiersmen all came together. The west was not always a safe place. There was very little justice and even less law in these savage lands.

Out here the law of the land was the rule and he who had the fastest gun arm made the law. It was a time of cowboys and indians, hustlers and land barons, thieves and bandits, and heroes and villains.

The Old West was the place where legends were made. These brave men and women who stood against the decadence and lawlessness would symbolize the most noble of human traits.

These brave souls stood against the corruption. Always outnumbered, they fought on to tame the Wild West.

If only one of those brave lawmen of legend had come to the town of Broken Eagle, perhaps life would have been better for the townsfolk.

Of course, if the law came to Broken Eagle it better be prepared for a fight.

This is the story of the greatest event in Broken Eagle's history.

This is the story of the Showdown at Broken Eagle.

SPECIAL THANKS!

As usual, none of this happens in a vacuum and there are some folks I'd like to single out for a BIG THANK YOU or twelve for helping get this 85 North ROAD TRIP started!

A BIG Thank You to John and the staff at Falstaf Books for inviting me to join the party. They are putting out some great books. Like Hartness says, you should buy their shit. It's good.

Also, BIG BIG THANKS to my Patrons who support my work on Patreon. I appreciate your continued support. John Nacinovich, Robert McIntyre, Carie Varner, John Kilgallon, James Burns, Jeff Allen, and Shantala Kay Russell. You guys rock!

Join me on Patreon at www.patreon.com/bobbynash

ABOUT THE AUTHOR

BOBBY NASH is an award-winning author of novels, comic books, short stories, novellas, graphic novels, and the occasional screenplay for a number of publishers and production companies. He is a member of the International Association of Media Tie-in Writers and International Thriller Writers.

Bobby was named Best Author in the 2013 Pulp Ark Awards. Rick Ruby, a character co-created by Bobby and author Sean Taylor also snagged a Pulp Ark Award for Best New Pulp Character of 2013. Bobby has also been nominated for the 2014 New Pulp Awards and Pulp Factory Awards for his work. Bobby's novel, Alexandra Holzer's Ghost Gal: The Wild Hunt won a Paranormal Literary Award in the 2015 Paranormal Awards. The Bobby Nash penned episode of Starship Farragut "Conspiracy of Innocence" won the Silver Award in the 2015 DC Film Festival.

For more information on Bobby Nash please visit him at www.bobbynash.com